Presented to _Alice Twomley-McIntyre_

From _Mom & Dad_

Occasion _Birthday_

Date _Nov. 5, 1998_

Dad
IN MY HEART

Compiled and Edited by

JOE L. WHEELER

 Tyndale House Publishers, Inc.
WHEATON, ILLINOIS

Visit Tyndale's exciting Web site at www.tyndale.com

Woodcut illustrations are from the library of Joe L. Wheeler.

Published in association with the literary agency of
Alive Communications, Inc.
1465 Kelly Johnson Blvd., Suite 320
Colorado Springs, CO 80920.

Library of Congress Cataloging-in-Publication Data

Dad in my heart / [compiled by] Joe L. Wheeler.
    p. cm.
    ISBN 0-8423-0556-4
    1. Fathers and sons—Literary collections. 2. Fathers and
daughters—Literary collections. 3. Father figures—Literary
collections. 4. American literature—20th century. 5.
Teachers—Literary collections. I. Wheeler, Joe L., date.
PS509.F34D33 1997
813.008′03520431—dc21
                                                    96-47578

Printed in the United States of America

03   02   01   00   99   98   97
7   6   5   4   3   2   1

DEDICATED TO
Lawrence Anthony Wheeler

My father is the rock of
faithfulness, steadfastness, and integrity
who inspired me to put together
this collection of stories.

CONTENTS

Acknowledgments ix

Introduction: Fathers on Castors xi
Joseph Leininger Wheeler

The Yellow Shirt 1
Joan Marie Cook

As a Grain of Mustard Seed 7
Hattie H. Carpenter

Their Word of Honor 19
Grace Richmond

What My Daughter Taught Me about Love 27
Robert Fulghum

The Question 31
Margaret E. Sangster Jr.

The Soul of a Violin 39
Ruth Lees Olsen

The Campus Ghost 47
Josephine DeFord Terrill

Tenderly and Forever 53
Author Unknown

A Lesson in Forgiveness 61
T. Morris Longstreth

At Home 71
Winifred Kirkland

Are You Going to Help Me? 77
Mark Victor Hansen

Dodsworth's Beans 79
Vincent G. Perry

Dad Walters' Son 87
Louise Gentry

Wedding by the Sea 93
Arthur Gordon

To the Victor 99
Alice Gorton Wynn

The Tiger 105
Mary Dirlam

Kathleen's Gold Piece 111
Christine Whiting Parameter

The Snob 119
Morley Callaghan

The Hidden Talent 123
D. B. Murphy Jr.

Who Said Rats? 127
Lewis Caviness

The Window Tree 133
Joan Marie Cook

Christmas Gift for Dad 137
Mary Sherman Hilbert

There's a Wideness 141
Joseph Leininger Wheeler

ACKNOWLEDGMENTS

"Introduction: Fathers on Castors," by Joseph Leininger Wheeler. © 1996. Printed by permission of the author.

"The Yellow Shirt," by Joan Marie Cook. Excerpted from *The Window Tree and Other Stories*, by Joan Marie Cook, © 1960 by Review & Herald Publishing, Washington, D.C. Reprinted by permission of the author.

"As a Grain of Mustard Seed," by Hattie H. Carpenter. If anyone can provide knowledge of the earliest publication and date of this old story, please relay the information to Joe L. Wheeler, in care of Tyndale House Publishers.

"Their Word of Honor," by Grace Richmond. Published in *The Youth's Instructor*, June 12, 1934, and in *Their Word of Honor and Other Stories*, © 1940 by Review & Herald Publishing, Takoma Park, Md. Text used by permission.

"What My Daughter Taught Me about Love," by Robert Fulghum. Excerpted from *It Was on Fire When I Sat Down on It*. Published in *Parade*, Sept. 10, 1989; and in *Reader's Digest*, Oct. 1989; © 1988, 1989 by Robert Fulghum. Reprinted by permission of Villard Books, a division of Random House, Inc. In the United Kingdom and British Commonwealth, reprinted by permission of Grafton/Harper Collins Publishers, Ltd., London.

"The Question," by Margaret E. Sangster Jr. If anyone can provide knowledge of the earliest publication and date of this old story, please relay the information to Joe L. Wheeler, in care of Tyndale House Publishers.

"The Soul of a Violin," by Ruth Lees Olsen. Published in *The Youth's Instructor*, Jan. 2, 1934, and in *Red Letter Day and Other Stories*, © 1942 by Review & Herald Publishing, Takoma Park, Md. Text used by permission.

"The Campus Ghost," by Josephine DeFord Terrill. Published in *The Youth's Instructor*, Sept. 24, 1935. Text used by permission.

"Tenderly and Forever." Author and original source unknown. If anyone can provide knowledge of the origins of this old story, please relay the information to Joe L. Wheeler, in care of Tyndale House Publishers.

"A Lesson in Forgiveness," by T. Morris Longstreth. Published in *The Youth's Instructor*, Feb. 10, 1925, and in *Their Word of Honor and Other Stories*, © 1940 by Review & Herald Publishing, Takoma Park, Md. Text used by permission.

"At Home," by Winifred Kirkland. Published in *The Youth's Instructor*, Jan. 13, 1914. Text used by permission.

"Are You Going to Help Me?" by Mark Victor Hansen. Excerpted from *Chicken Soup for the Soul: 101 Stories to Open the Heart and Rekindle the Spirit* by Jack Canfield and Mark Victor Hansen, © 1993 by Jack Canfield and Mark Victor Hansen. Used by permission.

"Dodsworth's Beans," by Vincent G. Perry. Published in *The Youth's Instructor*, Oct. 7, 1924. Text used by permission.

"Dad Walters' Son," by Louise Gentry. Published in *The Youth's Instructor*, May 19, 1931. Text used by permission.

"Wedding by the Sea," by Arthur Gordon. © 1974 by Arthur Gordon. Published in *Reader's Digest*, May 1974. Reprinted by

INTRODUCTION

Fathers on Castors: The Disappearing Father in America Today

JOSEPH LEININGER WHEELER

I have known colleagues who were always being reassigned, given new portfolios; rarely would they be doing the same thing they had been doing the previous year. When speaking of them, we'd sometimes quip, "Well, it's a good thing his/her walls are on castors." In retrospect, I'm a bit ashamed of our put-downs; I don't imagine the humiliation of continual reassignments was very funny to the person involved.

Today in America it appears that all too often fatherhood is on castors. The walls are moved so often that foundations appear irrelevant. With one of every two marriages ending in divorce, with multiple marriages and divorces all too common, with one in three children born out of wedlock in America today, fatherhood is increasingly treated as merely another throwaway.

I'll never forget what she said, that coed three or four years ago, when she and I were philosophizing outside my classroom. A child happened to toddle by, and her face softened: "Oh! Isn't he *cute?* . . . I want a boy too. Lots of them!" Then her facial expression changed, grew more rigid. "But I don't want a husband hanging around! Just long enough to give me a baby or two. I won't need him anymore after that."

I just stood there with my mouth open, unable to believe what I had heard. This was not a girl off the streets; this was an intelligent, attractive young woman who was paying considerable tuition money in order to secure a Christian education!

I began listening more—*really* listening—to the discussions in my writing and literature classes. I noticed that, generally speaking, the males in my classes had not the temerity males of my generation had. To put it mildly, many were scared to death of the New Woman who sat in that circle, ready to pounce on the slightest provocation. Fortunately, they would reveal their inner thoughts to me in their journal entries, in my office, in the halls, on the commons, or on field trips: "But, Dr. Wheeler, *please* don't ask me to express those feelings out loud in class. *They would eat me alive!*"

I shall never forget one assembly we had. The subject was "Women in History," and it was put on by coeds and women on our faculty. As the hour passed, the antimale rhetoric became increasingly virulent and nasty. It was unbelievably ugly.

Later on, I compared notes with male students who had been there, and I asked for reactions. What worried me then, and worries me now, is that while they shared my sense of outrage, unlike me they tended to just shrug it off as a terrible reality they felt powerless to change.

I also spoke with coeds who had been there and was encouraged to discover that many of them were almost as enraged as I. Since then I have discovered firsthand that many young women today are increasingly disturbed by what they perceive as feminism run amuck. They want men to exercise their God-given strength and leadership; to be there for them as potential mates, potential fathers of their children.

For most of this world's history, there has been a very clear demarcation between the male and female roles. The model, that of the Old Testament, is authoritarian and chauvinistic. Christ struck a much softer note in the New Testament, revealing to us a loving and caring attitude prior to then considered feminine rather than masculine. Thus the two Testaments combine for the first time the qualities God built into women and those He built into men. First Corinthians 13 is a long way from some of the bloody sagas of ancient Israel!

Almost alone among world religions, Christianity has elevated *both* sexes rather than just males. Love and romance as we know them cannot even be adequately portrayed in a society where women are second-class citizens.

God created us male and female, with both father and mother created in His image and thus both essential for procreation and preparation for life. When a man or woman attempts to fill both roles, neither ends up being filled very well. We are so complexly made that feminine traits without the masculine create wimps and masculine traits without the feminine create barbarians. One person cannot possibly do justice to both.

Whatever reservations I may have about Louis Farrakhan, I was profoundly impressed with his Million Man March on Washington, D.C. The message was loud and clear: It is high time for men to assume their God-given roles as husbands and fathers. We are hearing the same urgent message from the leadership of the Promise Keepers movement.

Thirty-some years ago, I heard a sermon that somehow managed to wedge itself into my conscious memory instead of gradually sinking into the murky depths of my subconscious. It has stayed there all through the years, being continually reinforced by sociological realities.

The place was Camino, California. The speaker was Pastor Royer. The message was this: Our perception of fatherhood has *everything* to do with our Christian walk with God. Royer illustrated it this way: Let's say that we are blessed with a strong, kind, caring, loving, Christian father whose marriage to our mother is for life. We grow up secure, loved, appreciated, believing in our own unique gifts.

We grow up loving our father—unconditionally—just as he loves us. Because of that firm foundation, we can love and trust a teacher or a preacher as a second father, mentors as surrogate fathers, law-enforcement officers as father figures, and government officials as parental figures deserving of respect. When a woman from such a background marries, she can respect her husband in the same way she respected her father.

But more important even than all this: We are able to love and respect God (the Trinity) as an extension of our earthly father concept. Because of this deep and abiding love and respect for our earthly father, we find it natural to love and respect God and achieve a close walk with Him.

On the other hand, went on Royer, let's suppose that our father was an alcoholic, a drug addict, one who battered us and our mother, one who seduced us as children and thus destroyed our innocence and self-worth, one who walked out on the family and left Mother to struggle alone in desperate poverty.

Now when we are told that a teacher is like a father, a minister is like a father, and so on about a policeman, a judge, a senator, a governor, a husband . . . what then? Clearly, we don't have to search far for the answer. We are terrified of all of them! We don't trust *anyone*.

Not even God! "God is like a father," we are told—and all we can think of is the hell we endured at home; hence we will perceive God Himself as demonic!

What an awesome responsibility for us fathers! To realize that our son or daughter will perceive all other men—and even God Himself—as but extensions of us. That we have within our power the ability to bless or blight every relationship our child will have in life.

What an important time for fathers (and fathers to be) to have role models, exemplars, patterns to follow. Men have been freed to care, to minister, to be sensitive, to be empathetic. But attempting the awesome responsibility of fatherhood without the daily transfusion of support, energy, and wisdom from our heavenly Father is the most futile of Sisyphian tasks.

The stories in this collection reveal the many faces of fatherhood, the qualities a father should have . . . to a generation that is in short supply of the genuine article. The stories showcase not only literal fathers but spiritual fathers—mentors—as well. And they also give real insights into the love of the heavenly Father of us all. It is my hope that these stories will have such God-given power that they can help to remove the castors under fathers' feet.

STORIES ABOUT FATHERS AND MENTORS

We do not internalize abstractions very well. They slide off the slippery sides of our memory and are seen no more. Not so with stories. If you want to rivet a child's attention on what you say, all you have to do is preface it with four simple little words: "Once upon a time. . . ." As if coated with Velcro, stories *stick!* And they don't go away. They, unlike ephemeral abstractions, doggedly dig into conscious memory and then keep digging until they reach our subconscious memory, not stopping until they tunnel into the subterranean bastion of our heart and the celestial eyrie of our soul. Once they reach these chambers, they dig no more, for henceforth they are part of us, part of our motivations, part of all that we think and say and do.

The tragedy of today is that millions of parents are willy-nilly in permitting revolting, obscene, and anti-Christian stories to dig their way into these two most sacred chambers of their children's being, there to determine their earthly and eternal destinies. The typical day's media fare, geared as it is to the lowest possible denominator, is virtually guaranteed to destroy all that is good, all that is idealistic, all that is *agape* loving in the child. Don't get me wrong: The media is not *all* immoral—there are a number of inspirational, informative, and educational shows on TV. But in proportion to all else, they are *so few!* Turn the TV on at any hour of the day or night and channel-surf, only this time metaphorically place yourself in the mind and heart of an innocent child who still retains illusions, then respond from that vantage point to all that you see and hear. We have become so used to television that we have long ceased to really pay attention to what it is saying, what it is showing. A living fulfillment of Pope's immortal epigram:

Vice is a monster of so frightful mien,
As to be hated needs but to be seen;
Yet seen too oft, familiar with her face,
We first endure, then pity, then embrace.

I urge you this day to *really listen to, really watch,* what is coming out of that handsome glass-eyed box in your home. When you have done so, I submit that, whether or not there are children in your home, you will realize that you yourself—whatever your age— are being changed just as certainly as would a child by what is being portrayed. None of us is *ever* home free! I am always in a state of becoming, as Tennyson put it in his immortal poem *Ulysses,* " a part of all that I have met."

In other words, I am the sum total of all that I have been exposed to. And *we* adults determine what we are exposed to and have the God-given responsibility to protect the avenues to the souls and hearts of our children, to shield them from the taboos of our society until they are mature enough to handle them without being destroyed in the process. It is long past time that we conquer our fatal inertia and fight back at the dark power which has made us all prisoners of fear, cowering in terror behind triple-locked doors and expensive burglar-alarm systems.

The government can't stop it, the police can't stop it, the schools can't stop it, even the churches can't stop it. No, the only power on earth that can . . . is the *home.* Within these walls, especially during those crucial first six years (when a child learns half of what will be learned in his or her lifetime), we parents can *begin,* at least, to stop it. We may not be able to single-handedly change society, but we *can,* with God's help, light a candle that will make of our erstwhile dark house a new beginning, a counter-force, if you will.

How can we do this? Simply by substituting eternal values for the media's primarily poor ones.

Because we learn through stories; because we internalize them; and because they then become part of our character—who we are, how we treat people, how we relate to our Lord—should we not, every precious day we have our children with us, share the kind of stories with them that can help to create valuable character traits? Nothing I have discovered creates a stronger bond than reading stories to a child on your lap or snuggled at your side. What a tragedy, then, that we do it so seldom!

But . . . to do so presupposes an almost inexhaustible supply of the right kind of stories. Not just the right kind, but ones that are virtually impossible to put down once you start reading them. Stories that keep you reeling back and forth between laughter and tears; stories that, once read, are so moving that you can never forget them and thus beckon you to return to them again and again. Where in the world does one find such stories?

WHERE THESE STORIES CAME FROM

I was lucky, wonderfully lucky. No, *lucky* is not the right word. I am convinced, beyond the shadow of a doubt, that even before I was born God had ordained me for this "ministry" of collecting and preserving wonderful old Judeo-Christian stories. You see, as a child of missionaries in Latin America, I was homeschooled by a remarkable mother, Barbara Leininger Wheeler. Mother was, and is, an elocutionist of the old school, one who memorized hundreds and hundreds of poems, readings, and stories—and who recited them often to church and school groups.

One never merely listened to Mother; her deliveries were virtual reality! Never a word mispronounced or misenunciated. One moment Mother would have people rolling on the floor laughing and the next, soaking a handkerchief with tears. And when she was through—a lump in the throat, new insights into life.

It took me many years to realize that God had set me up, had led me into the teaching of English and the collecting of stories—the old-timey stories I had grown up on. Through the years, I read them to my captive audiences (students in my classes); from their responses, I learned which stories had withstood the test of time and which had not.

In this countdown to the millennium, I am convinced that people everywhere are taking stock of themselves and their families, observing the collapse of the family and society, and seriously and prayerfully addressing the issue. That they are weighing the secular media in the tribunal of their mind and finding it wanting. That they are searching for values, the God-centered values this nation once had, which internalized, created the greatest democracy the world has ever known.

And they'll be looking for stories that have the power to transmit those values to our next generation, the first that will grow into maturity during the twenty-first century.

It was about five years ago that the Master Choreographer of the Universe apparently decided it was time to reassign me, time to entrust a bigger classroom—a much bigger classroom—to me. The result was *Christmas in My Heart*, a collection of my favorite Christmas stories. At the conclusion of my introduction, I asked for reader input; that if they felt so inclined, they could keep my feet to the fire by sending me their favorite stories, the ones that had meant the most to them and their families over the years. They *did* feel so inclined, and the mail has flooded in upon me and my wife, Connie, in wave after wave after wave. Thus, at the end of five years of anthologizing, I have more wonderful unused stories to choose from than I had at the beginning! The good Lord knew that no one or two persons alone could possibly find all the great stories needed to keep such a story ministry going!

So where have I found the greatest such stories? During the period I label "The Golden Age of Judeo-Christian Stories," from approximately 1880 to the mid-1950s. Many of these wonderful old stories have already disappeared forever; others are crumbling into dust as I write these words. There is not a moment to lose in seeking them out and helping to preserve them so they may bless generations yet unborn.

The fatherhood stories chosen for this book, by the way, are stories I have been collecting all my life. Some I heard as a child; others I found along the way; some are recent, but most were written during that incredible Golden Age I just referred to. I'm confident that when you read them you will see why I have such a determination to seek out and save the best ones from extinction.

CODA

So let me know your reactions to these stories and what new genre collections you would like to see us come out with. And do send us your favorite stories, making every effort to find the story's authorship and original date and place of publication, if you can. Each submission counts as a vote in terms of inclusion in a future collection. You may reach me by writing to:

Joe L. Wheeler, Ph.D.
c/o Tyndale House Publishers, Inc.
P.O. Box 80
Wheaton, IL 60189-0080

May the Lord bless and guide the ministry of these stories in your home.

The Yellow Shirt

JOAN MARIE COOK

Teachers—really great teachers—know their students. Not just superficially but deep down. And they love them. Teachers, who carry with them from moment to moment, day to day, week to week, month to month, and year to year, the awesome power to nurture towards self-sufficiency and greatness or shrivel into low self-esteem and nothingness. They are the fathers, the mothers, that bridge from home to the setting up of new homes in the adult world.

The movie Forrest Gump *brought home the rather startling concept that even those saddled with a low IQ are worthy of being treated with kindness and consideration. This is just such a story.*

This unforgettable true story is from Cook's one-of-a-kind little book, The Window Tree, *published in 1960.*

So this was my first college history class. The instructor walked in. He wore a shockingly yellow shirt and sat on the edge of the desk. He did not do our textbook the courtesy of opening it; instead he spoke to us, the students, of ourselves. He laughed often, and I thought I had never heard such a loud, uninhibited laugh. Professor Jackson's laugh amazed me almost as much as did his shirt.

History, to me, had always seemed to be too much involved with wars. A war, a war, and a war—with nothing in between but causes and effects. I was not prepared to enjoy a course in history.

Then, in the second week of the course, Professor Jackson assigned seats. Not alphabetically, but according to some secret scheme of his own, he lined us up by the blackboards and assembled us into rows. On one side of me was Nola Jeraldine Kirby, from "up in the mountains, close to Higginsburg," she told me. And on the other side, in immaculate "bucks" and hand-knitted argyles, sat Thomas Webb Carpenter. I knew this, *not* because he ever spoke to me to tell me, but because that was the name I saw on his neatly folded papers on their way to the aisle. I knew about his shoes because I was too awed by him for days to really turn and look at him, but I could see his shoes by moving just my eyes. After all, his entrance exams carried marks that had made him quite well known on our campus. He was a brilliant boy.

The history class was more than I had guessed a class could be—a constant interplay of ideas, an occasional jab of debate, enough joking so that everyone in the room felt quite at ease. Professor Jackson was one of those rare teachers who could allow this great amount of freedom in a class without ever losing his control over the situation or his dignity. I began to treasure the professor's cogent beginning-of-class prayers, his reverent examination of history in relation to the Bible. His whole *feeling* for history crept in around the edges of my thinking. After a while I rather liked his laugh; there was something free and unafraid in the heartiness, the very loudness of it. And the yellow shirt—well, he hadn't many others, so I learned to face it with a resignation that approached bravery.

The professor assigned a great deal of outside reading and more outside projects than most of us thought were necessary. My project partners—Nola and Mr. Carpenter of the immaculate bucks.

Meanwhile, Nola, to my left, struggled valiantly to condense the swift discussions into notes with her leaking, scratching pen and her cheap, cardboard notebook. And to my right, Thomas Webb Carpenter wrote his notes in flawless outline form without effort, without interrupting his own participation in a debate. Poor Nola, slow enough in any class competition when compared with my other neighbor, seemed even more painfully gross. I sometimes wondered if he ever saw her, noticed the way her plain, lonely face never changed from its strange, puzzled expression.

Sometimes when the topic was especially involved, Nola would glance at my notes and sigh. It was such a tiny, helpless sigh, and if I whispered, "Never mind, Nola, you just listen today, and I'll help you with your notes tonight," how she would smile at me.

We were in the library working on some map project, and I remember that the three of us were talking about what we would do after college. We were finished except for Nola, who was carefully coloring in a sea. Tom was telling us about his plans to become an engineer. His mother had insisted that he come to this college for at least a year, although he assured us he had no desire for the poverty connected with Christian service. Nola's hand, covered with small cuts and burns and stains from hours of work in the school kitchen, released its diligent grip on the crayon as she told us about the one-room building near her home where she wanted to start a school. "The church folks—they's all mighty anxious to help me get my two years' teacher training—no school a'tall for miles and miles up there. And the poor little children beyond Higginsburg, they don't have half a chance for growing up and meeting the world.

"I want 'em to have a real schoolroom like the one I got to go to when I stayed with my Aunt Jo, with real blackboards and a high shelf in the back to put their little lunch buckets on." She paused, her face flushed from so much unaccustomed talking. "I know you think I wouldn't be much of a teacher, because I'm not even what they call college material, but I'm all they got up beyond Higginsburg—and I love the children. Besides—" She leaned forward, and her face took on an intensity that surprised me. "Besides, the Lord helps me to remember just the things I need to know. Just ask my orientation teacher; it's supposed to be impossible for anyone with an IQ as low as mine to make grades as good as I do. The Lord just knows my purpose and helps me. I study very hard, but I couldn't make it without the Lord."

I had never heard anyone speak so honestly about his limitations before, and I was stunned. There was no joking in her manner, nor sullenness; she merely stated the facts. Even Tom Carpenter was disarmed. He looked at her for a long moment, and then he grinned and he said, "You'll make it, Nola. You really will. It's the spirit quotient that matters more than the intelligence quotient, and you'd rank genius there."

A dim smile crossed Nola's face. "The Lord helps me in all sorts of ways," she repeated simply. Then she picked up the blue crayon and went back to work.

The next day in class I saw Tom watching Nola as she took her pitiful notes. It was the first time I had seen him really observe anyone else. The next class period I noticed something strange at the desk to my right. Tom was bent over his notes, writing longer sentences, taking time with his words. When the closing bell rang, I saw him remove a carbon and give the extra copy to Nola. He only spoke to her for a moment, but somehow I couldn't linger to hear their conversation. During the weeks to follow, the extra set of notes became a regular procedure.

We all became such special friends—Tom, Nola, and I. One day when Nola made the highest score on a daily quiz, we all three nearly had to be sent from the room for laughing when, as we compared papers,

Nola said, "I'm sorry, Tom. I'll help you study your notes next time."

Every week Tom and I made a special trip to the library to find outside reading that wouldn't be too hard for Nola. And together the three of us studied for all major history exams, although it must have been a trial for Tom (he seemed actually to enjoy it). And Nola, when she worked behind the counter in the cafeteria, saw to it that the largest desserts were saved for Tom and me.

Sometimes I wondered how much of this odd three-way partnership had been planned in the secret mind of Professor Jackson, who never seemed

to notice what his seating arrangement brought about.

Tom and I talked of the professor once. Tom said, "Isn't it just beautiful the way that brilliant man brings his vast energies to focus in a classroom? His methods are subtle, but if you observe closely—he knows every person in each class very well. The questions he asks each one are the questions that person needs to answer or think about. I wonder how he does it."

"Why don't you ask him?" I ventured.

"Perhaps I will." There was silence for a long while, and each of us returned to his homework. Suddenly Tom said, "But I could never be a teacher. How could one live on that kind of salary?"

The idea of Tom Carpenter as a teacher left me speechless for a moment. "I don't know, Tom, about living on the salary. I suppose you'd just have to believe the way Jackson believes, that self-denial and happiness go together in a Christian's life."

"That's the answer, of course." And he took up his trig problems again.

January came with long, gray days of monotony. Semester exams were just behind us; no vacation in sight, too early for picnics, banquets, et cetera, to begin. January seemed the ebb tide of the school year. One evening Nola called me to her room after study period. She stood in front of the mirror trying to appear absorbed in making her hair stay in pin curls. "I want you to pray with me tonight because the business manager called me to his office today. I guess I have to go home on account of I can't work any harder than I am now, and I owe too much money."

"There must be some scholarship fund—"

"Not with grades like mine." She shoved her report card at me. Straight Cs except for a D in a math subject.

"I'll talk to him, Nola; I'll think of something. You just can't go home now when you're so near through."

She was crying now, and something in the quietness of her soft sobs, the rigid way she stood there, with the tears washing down her pale cheeks, showed how confused and afraid she was.

"Someone used to help me," she finally said. "I don't know who it was, but all last year and some this year, when things got pretty rough, someone would put some money in for me—sometimes just ten dollars, sometimes even fifty dollars. But this time, well, I just don't see any way out."

In my own room later I thought of Nola's progress—how painfully she had struggled with her grammar, how diligently she had studied her Bible lessons. What a beautiful lesson of faith she had been to me, for, just as she said, the Lord did know her purpose and did help her. Psychologists say that when it is difficult for a person to learn, it will usually be difficult for him to retain knowledge. This was not so in Nola's case. She remembered remarkably well. She constantly amazed her teachers. Then I began to wonder who had previously put money on her account. She didn't have many friends. Yet it must be someone who knew her fairly well, for who would put money to the credit of such a seemingly useless case unless he knew of her determination and dependence upon God?

The next day as I walked down a hall in the ad building, Professor Jackson walked out of the business office and joined me. There was a small slip of paper in his hand, which without notice he pushed into one of the books in the stack he was carrying. "I have something to tell you," he said, excitement sparkling in his eyes. "I just helped Tom Carpenter with his second-semester schedule."

"He's changing his major?" I asked.

"I thought you'd like to know," he said, unable to stop smiling. "I was never so pleased as when he came and told me. He's taking a double major—history and education."

I was as happy as the professor had expected. On the sidewalk when we said good-bye, he suddenly remembered a book he had for me. "Let's see, it's somewhere in this stack. I thought you might enjoy it for some outside reading," he explained, handing me a slim red volume of history in a period that particularly fascinated me.

In my room, when I opened the book, a small piece of paper fluttered to my desk. It was a receipt bearing that day's date. On it was written "Paid to the account of Nola Jeraldine Kirby, one hundred dollars."

It was weeks later in class one day that Nola whispered to me, "You know, I like that yellow shirt Professor Jackson has on."

I think she did not understand why there were tears in my eyes when I nodded my head and answered, "I think it's the nicest shirt I ever saw."

As a Grain of Mustard Seed

HATTIE H. CARPENTER

Peggy took the Bible's promises seriously. If all it took was to have faith no bigger than a mustard seed, then surely God would have to grant her modest request, for her faith that God would turn her into a boy during the night was total: there was no doubt at all.

When her prayer was not granted, and her world fell apart, it was poor Father who had to pick up the pieces.

Peggy knew just where to go for the mustard seed. She had helped gather greens from that end of the garden earlier in the summer. Nevertheless, after she had a number of the seeds in her hand, she broke off a piece of the stalk to carry to the house for identification. Peggy was a wise young woman, considering she had been in this world about eight speeding years.

The preacher had said with absolute conviction, "If ye have faith as a grain of mustard seed, ye shall say to the mountain, 'Remove hence to yonder place,' and it shall remove, and nothing shall be impossible unto you."

It was to obtain a correct idea of the size of a grain of mustard seed that Peggy had gone directly to the garden before she changed her Sunday dress. She had felt that a certain preparation was necessary for carrying out her important plans, plans that were to change all life for her.

Remembering now her Sunday dress, Peggy gazed down the length of it with much admiration. It was silk, a sky blue silk with ruffles and fancy pockets, and hand embroidered on the sash ends. The other girls in her class at Sunday school had called it "simply darling." And her leghorn hat and her white silk socks with tops blue like the dress.

The beauty of this raiment made her hesitate a moment. She would not have further use for it, if the faith she was planning to exercise should be applied at once. She might wait, she thought, until the dress was a few Sundays older, and she had forgotten and left her hat out in the rain, or somebody had sat on it, or something. But this was only the indecision of the moment. Resolutely purposeful, Peggy put the mustard seed into one of the little pockets and went back to the house and up the side stairs.

In her bedroom she arranged the dress very carefully on the hanger in the closet. She lingered there to smooth her hand over its silken texture. Her tones were deep with feeling when she said, "Good-bye, little beauty, good-bye. I'm never goin' to wear you again."

Out on the veranda Father was trying to elicit an account of the sermon from Lina, the baby of the family, and as soon as Peggy could get into her other clothes, she hurried to give assistance. Being two years older than Lina, Peggy naturally was better able to give reports of sermons and texts and things.

According to Peggy, the preacher not only had talked about faith moving mountains but had added: "If you are as good as you know how to be all the time and have faith the size of a mustard seed, you can have anything you want to have, do anything you want to do, go anywhere you want to go. If you ask, it will be given unto you."

The Sunday afternoon slipped away in the Granville home most peacefully: the older children off with various friends, Grandmother dozing in her chair, Father and Mother talking a bit and reading a bit, Peggy playing dolls with Lina in unbroken, even excessive, amiability.

Indeed, Peggy was more than good-natured. She was amazingly sweet. At the evening meal this was so noticeable it attracted general attention, for she voluntarily gave Lina the wishbone, and her "Thank you very much" and her "Pardon me, please" came so frequently that they gave Beth and Constance the giggles.

At seven thirty, instead of waging her usual fight for permission to go with the older children for the neighborhood game of gray wolf, Peggy took the astonished Lina by the hand and led her off to bed, singing softly as she went, "Two little hands to work for Jesus."

Halfway up the stairs, she looked down into the living room. How changed everything would be the next day. What amazement in that household when she descended these stairs in the morning.

In her pocket she fingered the grain of mustard seed. A tiny thing it was. She rolled it between her thumb and finger. Anybody could have faith as big as that.

Getting ready for bed, Peggy did all the things a careful child should do. She brushed her straight hair fifty licks. She scrubbed her teeth. She even helped Lina in a way that almost proved too much for Lina's curiosity.

"You're tellin' yourself a story," Lina cried. "That's what you're doin', Peggy. You're mean not to tell me, too."

"No," Peggy answered with a beautiful smile. "It is not a story. It's a truth." And after they were in bed, the story Peggy gave was a solemn rendition of the Shepherd's Psalm. Lina fell asleep.

"If you ask, it will be given unto you. . . . I shall not want." It was all very beautiful. Peggy had her eyes closed, thinking of these wonders and laying out her plans, when Judy—who still thought she was Peggy's nurse—came in and laid out Monday's clothes on the chair by the bed. That pink-and-white gingham, probably (Peggy smiled to herself)—that one with the cross-stitch trimming.

After doing something to the windows, Judy went

quietly out. Then Peggy slipped out of bed and crossed the room to her doll's cradle, showing plainly in the moonlight, and knelt beside it while she spoke softly.

"You may have brains I don't know about," she said, peering anxiously into the doll's sleeping face. "You may have human feelings. . . . If you have, Princess, I am sorry for the things I've said to you and for the way I've banged you around. I've been supposed to be your mother 'n' I ought to have done better by you. I'll try to look after you a little anyhow."

Standing then in the moonlight, her eyes carrying the exalted look of a St. Cecilia—who brought the angels from the sky—Peggy made her prayer. Her faith, her strong little heart told her, was greater than a mountain of mustard seed. She would ask, and "nothing would be impossible" to her.

Her two hands finger to finger in reverent supplication, her face upturned to look straight into the very gates of heaven, back of the shining stars, Peggy stood a moment in silence. Then gently, lovingly she said:

"Dear God, turn me into a boy tonight. On the chair where Judy put my clothes, please have a Boy Scout suit, a Sam Brown belt, a big jackknife, brown-and-blue plaid stockings, and knobby-toed shoes. (I wear elevens.) If You can fix it without too much trouble, please have some teeth come in where my front ones are out, and make my hair curly like Lina's. And, O Lord, I'll sing unto Thee a new made song. Thy mercy endureth forever."

She had not figured on these last two sentences, but when she went to bed she felt she had added a churchly note. One that surely had carried her prayer straight up into the hands of God. Sleepily she wondered about those hands of God—if they were as large as a world or the size of Father's, which were pretty big for a man. How Father would stare at her when she came down to breakfast. "Phillip" they'd probably call her on account of the *P* on her napkin ring.

After a while, her thoughts were too jumbled to make sense. Then the morning sun dazzled her awake. Someone was calling, "Time to get up, girlies," and instantly she remembered. Covering her eyes with her hand, she smilingly murmured, "Faith as a grain of mustard seed. Thank you, dear God," and looked.

There on that chair was the pink gingham dress. (There were the lace trimmed panties, the pink-topped socks, the black patent pumps.) God had not answered her prayer.

What could it mean? What could have happened? Peggy blinked back the tears. She must study this out somehow. She had had the faith, all right—something else was the matter. Perhaps, her cheeks hot at the thought, she had not been a good enough child to get her prayer a hearing. That was it—she was not good enough.

Ashamed, grief-stricken, Peggy found it difficult to swallow her food at the breakfast table, but she ate what was set before her, as nice children do. She did promptly, eagerly, everything she was told to do, and constantly looked for tasks to perform that might win merit on the angel's record book. All the day she was so very gentle, so surprisingly tractable that Mother took her temperature and looked at her tongue; Peggy found it wonderfully comforting, too, that evening to sit on Mother's lap, cuddled close in Mother's arms, and hear her say to Father, "This child, Fred, has been a perfect angel today—almost too good."

"A perfect angel"—it was so encouraging, for Peggy had found the day of perfect behavior an eternity of time. When bedtime came again, she sighed with relief, and humbly, on her knees this time, she used no highfalutin words at all.

"God," she put this flatly, "it doesn't matter about the teeth and the curls. Just put the clothes and the knife on the chair."

Morning came. The girl clothes were there just as Judy had left them.

Again Peggy went to work being a useful child, with many of her best intentions turning out all wrong. Vigorous dusting of her father's desk, for instance, brought disaster; for in some fashion the tall bottle of red ink turned over. Her savings bank, which she generously dumped into the lap of a blind beggar down the street, had happened to have the surprise money in it. Grandmother's crystal pitcher she had broken when she was merely giving it an extra polish.

Through it all, Peggy was patient, gently resenting no injustice, accepting all reprimands humbly, even asking forgiveness for things for which she was not to blame. Then at last bedtime came.

Nerves frazzled, throat lumpy, wearily feeling that she had been laboring on this goodness work for years and years, Peggy made ready for bed that third night in oppressive silence. She had been good—good and long-suffering. She had more than earned recognition for righteousness.

And that mustard-seed faith. Peggy had one of the tiny things in the palm of her little hand—it would be ridiculous for anyone to have faith that small. And yet (Peggy was tremulous with excitement), it was a Bible promise that faith that big could remove mountains. She'd have no more of this foolishness. She would make her prayer plain this night.

Lying stiffly still, Peggy kept wide-awake, waiting for the troublesome household to settle down for the night. The clock struck ten. It struck eleven. She arose to dispatch her ultimatum.

"God." Her voice was low and stern. "Turn me into a boy tonight. I give You leave to make me a flat-headed, freckle-faced, lopsided boy. You can put on that chair the dirtiest, raggedest clothes ever was, only God, if You can read my heart, You're seein' I'm gettin' pretty mad. My faith was greater than a grain of mustard seed—I asked, believin' I— I—" She went to pieces sobbing. The Amen never did get said.

Morning came once more. Peggy was awakened by the sound of the breakfast bell. She crooked up her neck from the pillow. On the chair by the bed was a ruffled, blue lawn dress.

Judy was entering the room, saying Father was waiting—Father required everybody to be at the breakfast table on time.

"Hurry, Darling." Actually Judy was smiling.

"Hurry? Why?" Peggy answered, lying back hard on her pillow and looking at Judy with blazing eyes.

"Ah, come now, Sweetness. Be a good little girl."

"I won't!"

"Peggy!"

"An' I'm never goin' to be good again. I won't go to breakfast. I ain't a goin' to do nothing anybody wants me to do. I'm goin' to say 'hain't' and 'deveil' and 'bust' 'n' everythings. Everybody's liars 'n' I hate everybody! I hate everybody! I HATE EVERY-BODY! I—" Peggy was working up an enormously loud voice, but Judy had gone out and closed the door, going downstairs, Peggy knew, to try to have her excused from coming to breakfast; Judy was like that.

Now she was opening the door again. Peggy caught her father's words distinctly called up the lower hall: "Tell Peggy to come at once. She understands my rules."

Very well, she would go. A flying leap from the bed, and she was out of the room. The forbidden banisters provided tremendous momentum. She struck against the post at the bottom, *kerplunk*. She rolled off right in plain view of the family at the dining table. She dashed to her place and gave Lina's

curls a yank, as she passed, that brought a gratifying howl of pain. She scrambled into her own chair and took great gulps of milk with loud gurgles in her throat.

Glaring from Mother to Father and back again, she waited for their reprimands. They had not

seemed to notice her. She made her most terrible face, using her thumbs in her ears, and her fingers at her eyes and her mouth, to stretch them horribly. Only Lina paid the least attention. She tapped her drinking glass with her knife, *tat-atat tat-atat*, like the fat man did at the restaurant. Father was looking across at Mother talking about the new car he was going to buy.

"I didn't wash my face, Old Woman." This terrible way to address Mother would surely start something. "An' I'm almost nekked, almost nek-ked!" she shouted. "All I got on is my skin and my nightgown." No notice yet.

"I'm never goin' to church again," in a still louder voice. "I'm never goin' to school. I'm never goin' to mind anybody. I'm goin' to bust the parlor window."

They were all looking at each other, those smart-alec grown-ups, saying things to each other without speaking. They were intending to ignore her. She had been done that way before. Very well, she would do a little ignoring herself. She'd never speak to anyone again; she'd be as dumb as wood. A poached egg she speared at long distance was soft enough to splatter when it struck the tablecloth halfway to her plate. Even this brought no order to leave the table, so she left of her own accord, flipping over her chair with a satisfactory crash as she departed.

"Not now, Mother, not now." (Father thought she had not heard his low voice.) They were intending to wait for her to calm down and then try to make her

sorry. Uh-huh, she'd show them. She would not get sorry, never, so long as she lived.

"They are all trying to line with me," Peggy told herself as the morning advanced. "Here comes Grandmother, bringing some peppermint candy. I'll snatch it and cram it in my mouth all at once and crunch and crunch."

Accepting attempts at coddling with impudence and insult, enduring various kinds of punishment with stoicism or with tantalizing laughter, Peggy came to the end of another day. While Lina, kneeling, said aloud her little prayer, Peggy shrilly sang, "Maggots in the cornmeal, maggots in the bran," the hired man's favorite Army song.

Thursday and Friday she contrived even worse ordeals for the family. Saturday she unintentionally did everybody a good turn by hiding away; then, yielding to curiosity, she had obeyed her mother's summons to come and talk to the family doctor who had been asked to call that afternoon.

Peggy had formerly liked the gentleman quite well. Her measles and her chicken pox had been decidedly enjoyable because they brought the doctor every day. But life had changed. In reply to his silly inquiry as to the state of her health, Peggy gave him a level stare and said, "Very poorly, if that suits you."

Her mother's scandalized "Peggy!" was opening for a real scene. But Doctor Craig's laugh spoiled everything, one of those nasty grown-up laughs at things you say wrong—like when she said "chicken percolator," meaning the box that hatched Rachel's biddies.

Her worst faces and her effective flounce out of the room seemed almost futile somehow, and from the hall she heard him say, "Don't worry about the child. I'll drop in again this evening with a little psychoanalysis test . . . but I fancy it is worms."

"Worms!" Insult on top of desolation. Peggy was almost blindly groping her way by the time she reached the low loft back of the attic. She cowered there in the dark and tried to keep her sobs inaudible. How utterly terrible it all was. Those stars in the faraway sky that had made her want to be so good. That grain of mustard seed. God's promise given and broken. All the beauty of life ruined—gone—all that, and they would give her vermifuge.

Crying did not help; it just made her sick at her stomach. She believed she had been in the loft hours with nobody coming to look for her. It must be nearly night—they were probably all down on the veranda, hearing Father tell something funny, herself forgotten completely.

Peggy noticed how dirty her clothes were because of the dust in the loft, so she did not change them. She stopped, however, to bathe her face. No use giving anybody the satisfaction of seeing that she had wept. By sopping her head up and down in the basin, she got her hair to dripping nicely. It dripped all the way down the stairs and across the living room. It lay damp and stringy against her cheeks as she strode,

chin up, past the family on the porch and made her way to the terrace coping.

Children were forbidden to climb on the coping, and Peggy found it dizzy business. She hardly thought she could walk the ledge, so, seeing Father starting toward her, she pretended to be trying to tie her shoe, sitting down to do it. Father was probably intending to inflict upon her one of those parent's talks—very well, she too, would use some language.

"I say, Peggy." (This was a new note. Peggy became alertly wary.) "My new roadster has come; how'd you like to go fishing tomorrow? Just you and I?"

Fishing? Fishing on Sunday? Could anything be more heathenish? Peggy let her face be its vivid little self for the moment.

"Way to the river?" she asked. "Would we stay all day? Would we cook on a campfire? Can I dig the bait right now?" Curious how trembly she felt, and Father seemed trembly, too.

The family stayed out of the way pretty much. If Dr. Craig came, Peggy did not know it, and when Lina said her prayers that night, Peggy did not interrupt her, for she was sound asleep.

Sunday morning brought a curious state of affairs. Nora, the very crossest cook that ever lived, asked Peggy with actual politeness to supervise the packing of the lunch basket. Everybody was rushing around as if she were—well, a sort of queen or something. It seemed prudent to be suspicious of such things and doings, and by turning her head suddenly she thought she might catch them. But she found nothing whatever to cause her offense.

The fishing tackle and the lunch and Father were already in the car when Peggy had the idea about the clothes. With no word of explanation she rushed into the house and up the stairs. It did not take her long, and everybody looked positively flabbergasted when she appeared in the blue silk dress, the leghorn hat, and Grandmother's white kid gloves.

"Peggy," Mother was beginning.

"And I am going to wear them." Her even tone, her even eyes Peggy knew were a success.

"Yes, yes, dear missus." (Of course that would be Judy.) "See, I am putting these grand little rompers in the car for her. Peggy's a good little girl, and she's going to bring home a big fish."

Just for a moment that sort of choky feeling came. Perhaps they all meant well—it certainly was wonderful to get to go off alone this way with Father. "Maybe I'll put them on, Mother," she called from the car. "I—I hope you will have a nice nap this afternoon."

After you leave the downtown traffic, it is sixteen miles to the river. Peggy, back again in the mood of the week, sat bolt upright, silent. She was being worked again, "worked" like when Constance used to send her on errands and pretend to count until she had returned, to see how fast she could go.

Now this fishing trip! The tail of her eye had a view of Father's face. He was smiling to himself— smiling to himself and trying to look sad at the same time. He thought she was a joke.

Fathers probably thought all girls jokes. Why, right now (Peggy's eyes stung with tears) if she were a boy, Father would be saying, "Come, Son, try out this wheel; I think you are going to make a cracker-jack driver someday. . . . Shouldn't wonder if you break the record." If God had kept His promise— Peggy's face went brick red in the surge of her anger.

A miserable ride. After they reached the river bridge and turned off the highway into the shady woods road, it wasn't quite so bad.

It was very quiet in the forest, one of those sweet-smelling forests that make you want to breathe deep down, and the narrow road twisted about with the course of the river so that you had to travel the three miles almost as slowly as the new car would run in high.

Peggy saw the willow tree for quite a while before they reached it. She knew it was the one Father had described so often, the one that had fallen into the stream and kept on growing until from its roots another tree had reached a great height. Close to shore under the prostrate tree was where the bass and perch grew to enormous size.

It was becoming hard to keep remembering to be angry. By the time the car was parked a short distance from the willow and Father had the tackle out on the running board, Peggy felt as if she just must throw her arms around him and give a mighty hug. But he was getting something else from the back of the car. Those rompers!

"Hooray," he called in that voice grown-ups like to use to children. "Look, Peggy. What say to taking off that flumdiddly dress and putting on these men's clothes?"

"Men's clothes!" Crowning insult. She did not speak. She knew no possible words. Father stood there holding those rompers, and he was grinning. All right, she would do her own fishing. She would take all the bait, and hadn't she dug every worm?

Snatching the bait can, Peggy caught up Father's cherished rod and reel. She felt as if she were flying, she went so fast to the willow tree and out its horizontal trunk. Father called for her to wait, and he could just keep on calling. She went clambering among the branches to the very crown of the tree before she looked back. He had followed her to the first crotch. The tree was bobbing up and down. He had stopped calling.

Below her the water was swirling darkly. It would be sort of hard to bait a hook here. The pole was forever catching the branches. She gave it a good jerk. Something cracked. She was going down; the pole was gone. The little branches were giving way. She was treading about upon slimy things, tangles of slimy willow limbs under the water. The water sucked her in farther and farther. Once she thought the whole river gurgled in her ears as she went entirely under.

Occasionally she got a hold. One big cozy limb did not slip so much. Clinging to it, she could pull herself up a little. Her breath was coming funny. The tree kept moving strangely. She thought she heard Father calling. Once she cried his name. Once she thought he was struggling in that slimy tangle. His face—yes, that was Father's face and that was his long arm, his big hand. She could just let go. Father was there.

The next thing she knew was when she opened her eyes and looked straight up into Father's looking down into hers. His face was queerly white. He was holding her tight in his arms. He was talking as if she were a tiny baby . . . calling her "babykins," "Daddy's blessedest," and things like that. . . . It sounded just lovely.

They were on the grassy bank under the tree. Peggy gave a quick glance toward the water, then looked away. She mustn't show that she had been scared.

"Father," she said, her voice quite small and quivery, "that's an awfully wet river."

Father just held her more tightly.

"Father," again, "did you see me go?"

"Oh, yes, yes, Peggy . . . and the tree would not hold my weight . . . and the branches in the water were in my way . . . Oh, Peggy!" (This hugging was really nice.)

"I'd 'a' hated to stay down in those branches." Peggy's shudder was more than a cold rigor. "And I guess I'd 'a' gone to hell in a hurry."

"Peggy!"

"Well, God seems to be high-hattin' me." Peggy spoke flippantly in an effort to ease up this all-gone feeling she was having. "He promised me things, then wouldn't keep His word. He . . . tricked me. He . . ." Peggy gulped down a sob.

"And when did He do you that way, Darling?" Father's voice was so kind, it brought more lumps into Peggy's throat. She must snap out of this sniveling. She must not act like a baby. It was no use. Her grief broke forth in a passion of tears, and when she could talk—when her sobs were more like a little spasm down in her heart—she poured out the whole story of that awful week.

"I asked . . . believing," she concluded with a gulp. "I had faith bigger'n all the mustard seeds in the world."

Father was holding her closely. He was understanding every word she said.

She looked up into his face and saw tears on his cheeks. Tears on Father's cheeks? It left a dirty smudge where she wiped them away with her hand, but that was all right. . . . Father did not seem to know that he was crying. He was looking away off. . . .

"Thank You, God," she heard him say softly. "Thank You, God, for tricking Peggy."

"You see, Peggy," he said in a solemn voice, after he had set her farther out on his knees so that they could look at each other face-to-face. "Every night since you were born I have been thanking God for giving you to me. Every night I ask Him to keep my little girl, just my little girl. . . . I, too, looked up at the stars with faith; I, too, . . ."

"Father!" Peggy was seeing it all now. "And if I'd got my prayer, you'd 'a' been feeling like I've been feeling."

In proportion to his size, Father's feelings would even have been by far more dreadful than hers had been. The preacher said, "When a man loses faith in the Almighty, he curses God and dies."

And all this time poor God had been doing the best He knew how. Trying to keep Father from cursing and dying. He really had expected her to be of some help.

Yes, and right at this moment Father was likely catching his death of cold. Anxiously Peggy felt his ears and his nose (that is the way to tell if anyone is going to have a chill); then she spoke with brisk firmness.

It took quite a long time to travel back the winding woods road, there were so many things to see. They even lingered awhile to watch a flying squirrel and to listen to the great silence of the forest. And then as they swung into the wide highway, there was not a car in sight for as far as the eye could see, and Father said, "Peggy, this motorcar certainly is a humdinger. Get over here back of the wheel, Old Pal, and try her out. You must have a fast car of your own someday."

"Old Pal!" . . . He called her "Old Pal" . . . a fast car of her own! Peggy sat as tall as possible as she gripped the big wheel. With Father's foot on the accelerator, they went smoothly into twenty, thirty, forty! She laughed right out, but never once did she swerve that car. Ahead of them the broad straight highway went on and on. She was as fine a driver as anybody in the world. And she had wanted to be a boy.

"Father," she said pretty soon, a mature little chuckle in her voice, "wasn't I the limit when I was a kid?"

Their Word of Honor

GRACE RICHMOND

The word honor *is little used anymore—sad to say.*
Everything, *it seems, is for sale to the highest bidder. If*
offered enough, precious few will scruple for long—no
matter how much sorrow the choice will leave in its
wake.

It was not always this way. Only a few generations
ago, one's honor was a commodity worth more than life
itself. It was binding; it was sacred.

Some years ago, Grace Richmond (1886–1959), one
of America's most beloved writers, penned this memorable
story of a father and grandfather who decided it was
time to test the next generation.

THE president of the Great B. railway system
laid down the letter he had just reread three times and
turned about in his chair with an expression of extreme annoyance.

"I wish it were possible," he said slowly, "to find
one boy or man in a thousand who would receive
instructions and carry them out to the letter without
a single variation from the course laid down. Cornelius." He looked up sharply at his son, who sat at a
desk close by. "I hope you are carrying out my ideas
with regard to your sons. I have not seen much of
them lately. The lad Cyrus seems to me a promising
fellow, but I am not so sure of Cornelius. He appears
to be acquiring a sense of his own importance as
Cornelius Woodbridge III, which is not desirable,
sir—not desirable. By the way, Cornelius, have you
yet applied the Hezekiah Woodbridge test to your
boys?"

Cornelius Woodbridge Jr. looked up from his
work with a smile. "No, I have not, Father," he said.

"It's a family tradition; and if the proper care has
been taken that the boys should not learn of it, it will
be as much a test for them as it was for you and for
me and for my father. You have not forgotten the day
I gave it to you, Cornelius?"

"That would be impossible," said his son, still
smiling.

The elder man's somewhat stern features relaxed,
and he sat back in his chair with a chuckle. "Do it at
once," he requested, "and make it a stiff one. You
know their characteristics; give it to them hard. I feel
pretty sure of Cyrus, but Cornelius—" He shook his
head doubtfully and returned to his letter. Suddenly
he wheeled about again.

"Do it Thursday, Cornelius," he said in his peremptory way, "and whichever one of them stands it shall go with us on the tour of inspection. That would be reward enough for anyone, I fancy."

"Very well, sir," replied his son, and the two men went on with their work without further words. They were in the habit of dispatching important business with the smallest possible waste of breath.

On Thursday morning, immediately after breakfast, Cyrus Woodbridge found himself summoned to his father's library. He presented himself at once, a round-cheeked, bright-eyed lad of fifteen, with an air of alertness in every line of him.

"Cyrus," said his father, "I have a commission for you to undertake, of a character which I cannot now explain to you. I want you to take this envelope"—he held out a large and bulky packet—"and, without saying anything to anyone, follow its instructions to the letter. I ask of you your word of honor that you will do so."

The two pairs of eyes looked into each other for a moment, singularly alike in a certain intent expression, developed into great keenness in the man, but showing as yet only an extreme wide-awakeness in the boy. Cyrus Woodbridge had an engagement with a young friend in half an hour, but he responded, instantly and firmly, "I will, sir."

"On your honor?"

"Yes, sir."

"That is all I want. Go to your room and read your instructions. Then start at once."

Mr. Woodbridge turned back to his desk with the nod and smile of dismissal to which Cyrus was accustomed. The boy went to his room, opening the envelope as soon as he had closed the door. It was filled with smaller envelopes, numbered in regular order. Enfolding these was a typewritten page, which read as follows:

"Go to the reading room of the Westchester Library. There open envelope No. 1. Remember to hold all instructions secret."

Cyrus whistled. "That's funny! It means my date with Harold is off. Well, here goes!"

He stopped on his way out to telephone his friend of his detention, took a Westchester Avenue car at the nearest point, and in twenty minutes was at the library. He found an obscure corner and opened envelope No. 1.

"Go to the office of W. K. Newton, Room 703, tenth floor, Norfolk Building, X Street, reaching there by 9:30 A.M. Ask for letter addressed to Cornelius Woodbridge Jr. On way down in elevator open envelope No. 2."

Cyrus began to laugh. At the same time he felt a trifle irritated. *What's father at?* he questioned, in perplexity. *Here I am away uptown, and he orders me back to the Norfolk Building. I passed it on my way up. He must have made a mistake. Told me to obey instructions, though. He usually knows just about why he does things.*

Meanwhile Mr. Woodbridge had sent for his elder son, Cornelius. A tall youth of seventeen, with the strong family features varied by a droop in the eyelids and a slight drawl in his speech, lounged to the door of the library. Before entering he straightened his shoulders; he did not, however, quicken his pace.

"Cornelius," said his father promptly, "I wish to send you upon an errand of some importance but of possible inconvenience to you. I have not time to give you instructions, but you will find them in this envelope. I ask you to keep the matter and your movements strictly to yourself. May I have from you your word of honor that I can trust you to follow the orders to the smallest detail?"

Cornelius put on a pair of eyeglasses and held out his hand for the envelope. His manner was almost indifferent. Mr. Woodbridge withheld the packet and spoke with decision: "I cannot allow you to look at the instructions until I have your word of honor that you will fulfill them."

"Is not that asking a good deal, sir?"

"Perhaps so," said Mr. Woodbridge, "but no more than is asked of trusted messengers every day. I will assure you that the instructions are mine and represent my wishes."

"How long will it take?" inquired Cornelius, stooping to flick an imperceptible spot of dust from his trousers.

"I do not find it necessary to tell you."

Something in his father's voice sent the languid Cornelius to an erect position and quickened his speech.

"Of course I will go," he said, but he did not speak with enthusiasm.

"And—your word of honor?"

"Certainly, sir." The hesitation before the promise was only momentary.

"Very well. I will trust you. Go to your room before opening your instructions."

And the second somewhat mystified boy went out of the library on that memorable Thursday morning, to find his first order one which sent him to a remote district of the city, with the direction to arrive there within three quarters of an hour.

Out on an electric car Cyrus was speeding to another suburb. After getting the letter from the tenth floor of the Norfolk Building, he had read:

"Take crosstown car on L Street, transfer to Louisville Avenue, and go out to Kingston Heights. Find corner West and Dwight Streets and open envelope No. 3."

Cyrus was growing more and more puzzled, but he was also getting interested. At the corner specified he hurriedly tore open No. 3 but found, to his amazement, only the singular direction:

"Take Suburban Underground Road for Duane Street Station. From there go to *Sentinel* office and secure third edition of yesterday's paper. Open envelope No. 4."

"Well, what under the sun, moon, and stars did he send me out to Kingston Heights for?" cried Cyrus aloud. He caught the next train, thinking longingly of his broken engagement with Harold Dunning and of certain plans for the afternoon which he was beginning to fear might be thwarted if this seemingly endless and aimless excursion continued. He looked at the packet of unopened envelopes.

It would be easy to break open the whole outfit and see what this game is, he thought. *Never knew Father to do a thing like this before. If it's a joke*—his fingers felt the seal of envelope No. 4—*I might as well find it out at once. Still, Father never would joke with a fellow's promise the way he asked it of me. "My word of honor"—that's putting it pretty strong. I'll see it through, of course. My, but I'm getting hungry! It must be near luncheontime.*

It was not; but by the time Cyrus had been ordered twice across the city and once to the top floor of a sixteen-story building in which the elevator service was out of order, it was past noon, and he was in a condition to find envelope No. 7 a very satisfactory one:

"Go to Café Reynaud on Westchester Square. Take a seat at table in left alcove. Ask waiter for card of Cornelius Woodbridge Jr. Before ordering luncheon open envelope No. 8 and read the contents."

The boy lost no time in obeying this command and sank into his chair in the designated alcove with a sigh of relief. He mopped his brow and drank a glass of ice water at a gulp. It was a warm October day, and the sixteen flights had been somewhat trying. He asked for his father's card and then sat studying the attractive menu.

"I think I'll have—," he mused for a moment, then said with a laugh, "Well, I'm about hungry enough to eat the whole thing. Bring me the—"

Then he recollected, paused, and reluctantly pulled out envelope No. 8 and broke the seal. "Just a minute," he murmured to the waiter. Then his face turned scarlet, and he stammered under his breath, "Why—why—this can't be—"

Envelope No. 8 ought to have been bordered with black, if one may judge by the dismay caused by its order to a lecture hall to hear a famous electrician speak. But the Woodbridge blood was up now, and it was with an expression resembling that of his grandfather Cornelius under strong indignation that Cyrus stalked out of that charming place to proceed grimly to the lecture hall.

Who wants to hear a lecture on an empty stomach? he groaned. *I suppose I'll be ordered out, anyway, the minute I sit down and stretch my legs. Wonder if Father can be exactly right in his mind. He doesn't believe in wasting time, but I'm wasting it today by the bucketful. Suppose he's doing this to size me up some way? Well, he isn't going to tire me out so quickly as he thinks. I'll keep going till I drop.*

Nevertheless, when he was ordered to leave the lecture hall and go three miles to a football field, and then was ordered away again without a sight of the game he had planned for a week to see, his disgust was intense.

All through that long, warm afternoon he raced about the city and suburbs, growing wearier and more empty with every step. The worst of it was, the orders were beginning to assume the form of a schedule and commanded that he be here at 3:15, and there at 4:05, and so on, which forbade loitering, had he been inclined to loiter. In it all he could see no purpose, except the possible one of trying his physical endurance. He was a strong boy, or he would have been quite exhausted long before he reached envelope No. 17, which was the last but three of the packet. This read:

"Reach home at 6:20 P.M. Before entering house, read No. 18."

Leaning against one of the big white stone pillars of the porch of his home, Cyrus wearily tore open envelope No. 18, and the words fairly swam before his eyes. He had to rub them hard to make sure that he was not mistaken:

"Go again to Kingston Heights, corner West and Dwight Streets, reaching there by 6:50. Read No. 19."

The boy looked up at the windows, desperately angry at last. If his pride and his idea of the meaning of the phrase, "my word of honor," as the men of the Woodbridge family were in the habit of teaching it to their sons, had not both been of the strongest sort, he would have rebelled and gone defiantly and stormily in. As it was, he stood for one long minute with his hands clenched and his teeth set; then he turned and walked down the steps away from the longed-for dinner and out toward L Street and the car for Kingston Heights.

As he did so, inside the house on the other side of the curtains, from behind which he had been anxiously peering, Cornelius Woodbridge Sr. turned about and struck his hands together, rubbing them in a satisfied way.

"He's come—and gone," he cried softly, "and he's on time to the minute!"

Cornelius Jr. did not so much as lift his eyes from the evening paper, as he quietly answered, "Is he?" But the corners of his mouth slightly relaxed.

The car seemed to crawl out to Kingston Heights. As it at last neared its terminus, a strong temptation seized the boy Cyrus. He had been on a purposeless errand to this place once that day. The corner of West and Dwight Streets lay more than half a mile from the end of the car route, and it was an almost untenanted district. His legs were very tired; his stomach ached with emptiness. Why not wait out the interval which it would take to walk to the corner and back in a little suburban station, read envelope No. 19, and spare himself? He had certainly done enough to prove that he was a faithful messenger.

Had he? Certain old and well-worn words came into his mind; they had been in his writing book in the early school days: "A chain is no stronger than its weakest link." Cyrus jumped off the car before it stopped and started at a hot pace for the corner of West and Dwight Streets. There must be no weak places in his word of honor.

Doggedly he went to the extreme limit of the indicated route, even taking the longest way round to make the turn. As he started back, beneath the arc light at the corner there suddenly appeared a city messenger boy. He approached Cyrus and, grinning, held out an envelope.

"Ordered to give you this," he said, "if you made connections. If you'd been later than five minutes past seven, I was to keep dark. You've got seven minutes and a half to spare. Queer orders, but the big railroad boss, Woodbridge, gave 'em to me."

Cyrus made his way back to the car with some self-congratulations that served to brace up the muscles behind his knees. This last incident showed him plainly that his father was putting him to a severe test of some sort, and he could have no doubt that it was for a purpose. His father was the sort of man who does things with a very definite purpose indeed. Cyrus looked back over the day with an anxious searching of his memory to be sure that no detail of the singular service required of him had been slighted.

As he once more ascended the steps of his own home, he was so confident that his labors were now ended that he almost forgot about envelope No. 20, which he had been directed to read in the vestibule before entering the house. With his thumb on the bell button he remembered, and with a sigh broke open the final seal:

"Turn about and go to Lenox Street Station, B. Railroad, reaching there by 8:05. Wait for messenger in west end of station."

It was a blow, but Cyrus had his second wind now. He felt like a machine—a hollow one—which could keep on going indefinitely.

The Lenox Street Station was easily reached on time. The hands of the big clock were at only one minute past eight when Cyrus entered. At the designated spot the messenger met him. Cyrus recognized him as the porter on one of the trains of the road of which his grandfather and father were officers. Why, yes, he was the porter of the Woodbridge special car! He brought the boy a card which ran thus:

"Give porter the letter from Norfolk Building, the card received at restaurant, the lecture coupon, yesterday evening's *Sentinel*, and the envelope received at Kingston Heights."

Cyrus silently delivered up these articles, feeling a sense of thankfulness that not one was missing. The porter went away with them, but was back in three minutes.

"This way, sir," he said, and Cyrus followed, his heart beating fast. Down the track he recognized the Fleetwing, President Woodbridge's private car. And Grandfather Cornelius he knew was just starting on a tour of his own and other roads, which included a flying trip to Mexico. Could it be possible—

In the car his father and grandfather rose to meet him. Cornelius Woodbridge Sr. was holding out his hand.

"Cyrus, lad," he said, his face one broad, triumphant smile, "you have stood the test, the Hezekiah Woodbridge test, sir, and you may be proud of it. Your word of honor can be depended upon. You are going with us through nineteen States and Mexico. Is that reward enough for one day's hardships?"

"I think it is, sir," agreed Cyrus, his round face reflecting his grandfather's smile, intensified.

"Was it a hard pull, Cyrus?" questioned the senior Woodbridge with interest.

Cyrus looked at his father. "I don't think so—now, sir," he said. Both men laughed.

"Are you hungry?"

"Well, just a little, Grandfather."

"Dinner will be served the moment we are off. We have only six minutes to wait. I am afraid—I am very much afraid—"the old gentleman turned to gaze searchingly out of the car window into the station— "that another boy's word of honor is not—"

He stood, watch in hand. The conductor came in and remained, awaiting orders. "Two minutes more, Mr. Jefferson," he said. "One and a half—one—half a minute." He spoke sternly. "Pull out at 8:14 on the second, sir. Ah—"

The porter entered hurriedly and delivered a handful of envelopes into Grandfather Cornelius's grasp. The old gentleman scanned them at a glance.

"Yes, yes—all right!" he cried with the strongest evidences of excitement Cyrus had ever seen in his usually quiet manner. As the train made its first gentle motion of departure, a figure appeared in the doorway. Quietly, and not at all out of breath, Cornelius Woodbridge III walked into the car.

Then Grandfather Woodbridge grew impressive. He advanced and shook hands with his grandson as if he were greeting a distinguished member of the board of directors. Then he turned to his son and

solemnly shook hands with him also. His eyes shone through his gold-rimmed spectacles, but his voice was grave with feeling.

"I congratulate you, Cornelius," he said, "on possessing two sons whose word of honor is above reproach. The smallest deviation from the outlined schedule would have resulted disastrously. Ten minutes' tardiness at the different points would have failed to obtain the requisite documents. Your sons did not fail. They can be depended upon. The world is in search of men built on those lines. I congratulate you, sir."

Cyrus was glad presently to escape to his stateroom with Cornelius. "Say, what did you have to do?" he asked eagerly. "Did you trot your legs off all over town?"

"Not much, I didn't!" said Cornelius grimly from the depths of a big towel. "I spent the whole day in a little hole of a room at the top of an empty building, with just ten trips down the stairs to the ground floor to get envelopes at certain minutes. Twice messengers met me unannounced at the top—checking up on me, I suppose, to see if I made it all the way back to that musty room. It was stifling hot there, too. I had not a crumb to eat or a thing to do and could not even snatch a nap for fear I'd oversleep one of my dates at the bottom."

"I believe that was worse than mine," admitted Cyrus reflectively.

"I should say it was. If you don't think so, try it."

"Dinner, boys," announced their father just outside their door—and they lost no time in responding.

What My Daughter Taught Me about Love

ROBERT FULGHUM

Life is funny, isn't it? None of us seems to agree on what is valuable in life and what is not. Worse yet, we are not even consistent ourselves: What we label worthless at one stage of our life we would almost kill for later.

Robert Fulghum, best known for his best-selling All I Really Need to Know I Learned in Kindergarten, *ruefully remembers a day when he flunked fatherhood.*

His life has never been the same since.

Neither—I would guess—will be the lives of those who read this story.

THE cardboard box is marked "The Good Stuff." As I write, I can see where it is stored on a high shelf in my studio. I like being able to see it when I look up. The box contains those odds and ends of personal treasures that have survived many bouts of clean-it-out-and-throw-it-away that seize me from time to time. It has passed through the screening done as I've moved from house to house and hauled stuff from attic to attic. A thief looking into the box would not take anything. But if the house ever catches on fire, the box goes with me when I run.

One of the keepsakes in the box is a small paper bag. Lunch size. Though the top is sealed with duct tape, staples, and several paper clips, there is a ragged rip in one side through which the contents may be seen.

This particular lunch sack has been in my care for maybe fourteen years. But it really belongs to my daughter, Molly. Soon after she came of school age, she became an enthusiastic participant in packing lunches for herself, her brothers, and me. Each bag got a share of sandwiches, apples, milk money, and sometimes a note or a treat. One morning, Molly handed me two bags. One regular lunch sack. And the one with the duct tape and staples and paper clips.

"Why two bags?"

"The other one is something else."

"What's in it?"

"Just some stuff—take it with you."

Not wanting to hold court over the matter, I stuffed both sacks into my briefcase, kissed the child, and rushed off.

At midday, while hurriedly scarfing down my real lunch, I tore open Molly's bag and shook out the contents. Two hair ribbons, three small stones, a plastic dinosaur, a pencil stub, a tiny seashell, two animal crackers, a marble, a used lipstick, a small doll, two chocolate kisses, and thirteen pennies.

I smiled. How charming. Rising to hustle off to all the important business of the afternoon, I swept the desk clean, into the wastebasket—leftover lunch, Molly's junk and all. There wasn't anything in there I needed.

That evening Molly came to stand beside me while I was reading the paper. "Where's my bag?"

"What bag?"

"You know, the one I gave you this morning."

"I left it at the office, why?"

"I forgot to put this note in it." She handed over the note. "Besides, I want it back."

"Why?"

"Those are my things in the sack, Daddy, the ones I really like. I thought you might like to play with them, but now I want them back. You didn't lose the bag, did you, Daddy?" Tears puddled in her eyes.

"Oh, no. I just forgot to bring it home," I lied. "Bring it tomorrow. OK?"

"Sure thing—don't worry." As she hugged my neck with relief, I unfolded the note that had not got into the sack: "I love you, Daddy."

Oh. And also—uh-oh.

I looked long at the face of my child.

She was right—what was in that sack was "something else." Molly had given me her treasures. All that a seven-year-old held dear. Love in a paper sack. And I had missed it. Not only missed it, but had thrown it away because "there wasn't anything in there I needed." Dear God.

It wasn't the first or the last time I felt my Daddy Permit was about to run out.

It was a long trip back to the office. But there was nothing else to be done. So I went. The pilgrimage of a penitent. Just ahead of the janitor. I picked up the wastebasket and poured the contents on my desk. I was sorting it all out when the janitor came in to do his chores.

"Lose something?"

"Yes, my mind."

"It's probably in there, all right. What's it look like, and I'll help you find it."

I started not to tell him. But I couldn't feel any more of a fool than I was already in fact, so I told him.

He didn't laugh. "I got kids too." So the brotherhood of fools searched the trash and found the jewels, and he smiled at me and I smiled at him. You are never alone in these things. Never.

After washing the mustard off the dinosaur and spraying the whole thing with breath freshener to kill the smell of onions, I carefully smoothed out the wadded ball of brown paper into a semifunctional bag and put the treasures inside and carried it home gingerly, like an injured kitten. The next evening, I returned it to Molly, no questions asked, no explanations offered. The bag didn't look so good, but the stuff was all there, and that's what counted.

After dinner I asked her to tell me about the stuff in the sack, and so she took it all out a piece at a time and placed the objects in a row on the dining-room table. It took a long time to tell. Everything had a story, a memory, or was attached to dreams and imaginary friends. Fairies had brought some of the things. And I had given her the chocolate kisses, and she had kept them for when she needed them. I managed to say "I see" very wisely several times in the telling. And, as a matter of fact, I did see.

To my surprise, Molly gave the bag to me once again several days later. Same ratty bag. Same stuff inside. I felt forgiven. And trusted. And loved. And a little more comfortable wearing the title of Father. Over several months, the bag went with me from time to time. It was never clear to me why I did or did not get it on a given day. I began to think of it as the Daddy Prize and tried to be good the night before so I might be given it the next morning.

In time Molly turned her attention to other things—found other treasures, lost interest in the game, grew up. Something. Me? I was left holding the bag. She gave it to me one morning and never asked for its return. And so I have it still.

Sometimes I think of all the times in this sweet life when I must have missed the affection I was being given. A friend calls this "standing knee-deep in the river and dying of thirst."

So the worn paper sack is there in the box. Left from a time when a child said, "Here—this is the best I've got—take it—it's yours. Such as I have, give I to thee."

I missed it the first time. But it's my bag now.

The Question

MARGARET E. SANGSTER JR.

Should one's past, one's mistakes—especially big ones—be made known to everyone? That was the question Dr. Barlowe faced with the engaged couple seated before him. And his dilemma was complicated by the fact that Elizabeth was like a second daughter to him. As a revered minister who had been like a father to the town for half a century, he had to think of the results should he not reveal the mistake.

So here he was in his study—after the couple had left—with his heartrending secret. What should he do?

Margaret E. Sangster Jr. (1894–1981), the granddaughter of the equally legendary Margaret E. Sangster Sr., wrote some of the most powerful and memorable inspirational stories our nation has ever known. This particular story—a natural companion piece to O. Henry's great story, "A Retrieved Reformation"—is virtually unknown today. What a joy it is to bring it back.

DR. BARLOWE'S kind old eyes were puzzled as he shook hands with the new cashier of the First National Bank.

"Somehow," he said, "—and it's not like me to forget; I have a good memory!—but somehow I feel that we've met before. The time and the place—they've quite gone from me. But somehow—" He hesitated.

John Murray returned the pressure of the minister's fingers. His eyes looked squarely into the minister's eyes. And—

"I don't think," he answered, "that we've ever met. I'm sorry. I should have enjoyed being your friend—through all my life. But, as you know, I've just recently come from the East—I've never been west before. And you—you've never lived in the East. Have you?" He smiled charmingly.

Dr. Barlowe answered. His tone was thoughtful.

"I've only been away twice from this State," he said, "and then I didn't get to the East, really. I was doing some speaking. The program of my lectures took me through a group of Middle Western towns and cities. But—well, it is curious. Your face seems so familiar—"

Again, just as charmingly as he had before, John Murray smiled. "It's going to grow more and more familiar to you as time goes on," he said. "You'll soon be tired of seeing this face in a front pew Sabbath after Sabbath."

Dr. Barlowe laughed and patted the younger man's shoulder. Already he liked this engaging chap from the East. The First National, he told himself, had made a wise choice. John Murray's smile was as good as another man's bond!

And as the days went on, others agreed with Dr. Barlowe. For unconsciously, the warmhearted Western town opened its arms to John Murray and gathered him in. Even the local young men—who had hoped for the coveted position that Murray filled in the bank—became his friends. "He knows the business," they said. "Maybe it's better for an organization to have new blood once in a while!" And then, in answer to questions, "Where's he from, you say? Really, we don't know. But he must have good credentials. And he's certainly on the job!"

Yes, the town took John Murray to its heart! He was invited to the best homes—to the most exclusive social events. The girls of the town were frankly flattered at the smallest attention that he paid them. The solid businessmen asked his advice on politics and the market. The young boys copied his cravats!

And still Dr. Barlowe, looking down into the young man's earnest, raised face every Sabbath, wondered where they had met before, if ever. Wondered why that lifted face had a way of touching, lightly, upon some chord of memory. Still, Dr. Barlowe, even as he extended his white old hands in the majesty of the benediction, asked himself if that lost chord of memory would ever ring out clearly across his mind.

During the first six months of his stay in town, John Murray was just a general favorite, mingling at will with everyone. But after the first six months, he began to specialize! During the daytime, of course, his hours were employed at the bank, at luncheon clubs, and with his business associates. But when evening came, his steps led him, with increasing frequency, toward a certain vine-covered cottage on a certain unimportant street. It wasn't long before people began to whisper of a budding romance. For in the vine-covered cottage lived the girl who played the organ in Dr. Barlowe's church. Dr. Barlowe, who had baptized her some twenty-odd years before, thought her the sweetest girl in town!

There were some who were surprised at John's choice—although the whole community shared Dr. Barlowe's opinion of the girl who lived in the cottage. There were some who said that John Murray might have done well to let his head rule his heart—for the bank's president had a pretty, unmarried daughter who had smiled on the young cashier from the East. The daughter drove a Cadillac roadster and wore expensive clothes. And more than once that roadster had been drawn up in front of the bank at the end of the day, at an hour when John was due to come out of the door and start toward his boarding house.

The town liked John the better because he had chosen a girl with no money—an orphan who earned a small living by the music that lived in her fingertips. But the town said that he might have married a million, if he had cared to do so.

Dr. Barlowe knew that the town was right. But he didn't care. For on the Sabbath after the engagement was announced, he saw John Murray's eyes raised to the choir loft, from which pealed the softness of an anthem. And he saw reverence in those eyes—reverence and something so close to agony that his heart seemed to turn over.

Love is like that, he said to himself and preached a new sermon without notes. A sermon about youth and hope and the coming of springtime. A sermon that had grown, as spontaneously as a flower, beneath the white flame in a young man's glance.

They came to call on him that afternoon in the

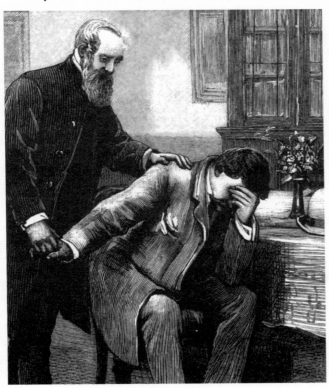

study. John Murray and the girl who played the organ in the choir loft. Dr. Barlowe always sat in his study on a Sabbath afternoon, and usually he had visitors. It was in this simple room, with its books and its worn desk, with its opened window through which the sun came pouring, with its low-branching trees beyond the window, that Dr. Barlowe played friend and father to his people. In that study cares were laid aside and responsibilities were taken up. In that study broken hearts were mended. In that study gallant vows were renewed, and old mistakes were forgiven and—yes, forgotten, as well.

Dr. Barlowe had known that John and the girl would come to him. Young people always came to him after an engagement had been announced. To talk of a marriage and a home to be. To receive his blessing.

John Murray? His smile was more winning than ever. The girl was radiant. Dr. Barlowe motioned them quietly to chairs—chairs near the window, so that he might better see their young faces in the sunlight.

It fell in bars through the branches of the trees outside, that sunlight. In bars across the girl's face—in bars across the face of John.

All at once Dr. Barlowe's trembling hand had crept up to touch his quivering mouth. He had remembered, at last, where he had seen John Murray before.

How he got through that talk with the newly engaged couple, Dr. Barlowe never knew. It seemed that they were in his study for hours—instead of a matter of minutes. It seemed as if the words that he spoke were utterly hollow. It seemed as if his suggestions about the wedding were quite unreal. Only he knew, with a sudden, burning intensity, that he must speak, alone, with John Murray. That he must speak alone, and at once! As the young people rose at last to leave, his shaking hand touched John's sleeve.

"I wish that you'd let Elizabeth" (it was the girl's name) "go home by herself, my boy," he said, with an attempt at lightness. "Just this once, by herself! I'd like to talk with you for a moment."

The girl laughed.

"Our pastor is like a real father to me, John," she said. "He's probably going to ask if you can support me in the style to which I've been accustomed." And then swiftly she had leaned forward and had laid her hand in Dr. Barlowe's.

"You dear," she breathed. And was gone.

And Dr. Barlowe, with a great lump in his throat making it almost impossible for him to utter words, turned to the other man. He didn't beat around the bush; that wasn't Dr. Barlowe's way!

"It was in prison that I saw you," he said, "on one of my speaking trips back in the Middle West. I preached at a State penitentiary. You were well in the back of the room—but I remember how you watched me, how you listened. I never forgot your face."

John answered wearily. "I always knew," he said, "that you would remember . . . sometime!"

Dr. Barlowe's voice was grave. But it was the gentlest voice in the world. "Suppose you tell me about it," he said. "*All* about it."

John Murray shrugged ever so slightly. The charming smile no longer played around his mouth. But the agony that Dr. Barlowe had glimpsed in his eyes had grown—until it filled those eyes. Dr. Barlowe knew now that it had not been entirely an emotion inspired by love.

"It was the usual thing," John Murray answered. "I was a foolish boy. I borrowed money from the bank in which I worked. Borrowed it, without asking, to speculate with. I don't suppose it matters that I needed money for my mother—she was ill, and an operation seemed necessary. Well—" he tried to keep his voice steady—"the stocks went down instead of up. I couldn't put the money back. And my mother died while I was away."

The young man's voice cracked sharply, steadied again, and went on. "I took courses while I was in prison," he said, "and there was a judge who grew interested in me. He gave me a job—when I got out. But it was of no use. People remembered. And so the judge suggested that I make a new start—in a faraway place. So I came west. He gave me a letter. I had no other credentials, but they were not very inquiring here. They took me at face value. And you—you were my only link to the past. For, of course, I—remembered—you. Only—" Suddenly the old smile, a trifle shaky, was back again. "Only I was sure, when you *did* remember, that you'd not give me away. That you'd help me—"

Help me! Dr. Barlowe was looking straight ahead as he answered. His very answer was a question.

"But is it helping you," he asked, "to aid you in living a lie? Wouldn't I be helping you more if I went with you while you told your story to the ones most interested? Elizabeth, I mean. She should know. And the president of the First National. And—"

But all at once John Murray was on his feet. And his burning eyes stared from an agonized, white face into Dr. Barlowe's eyes.

"Why," he asked, "should Elizabeth know? It would only hurt her faith in me. Why should the president know? It would only give him a doubt that he doesn't possess now. Elizabeth—oh, she loves me. She'd marry me, despite anything. But it wouldn't be the same. My job—they might not dismiss me. But the president might tell his wife, and his wife would tell their daughter. And his daughter—you know how some girls are—" Dr. Barlowe, too, was thinking of a certain young woman's shattered hopes. "Soon the town would know! And then—then it would be 'Jailbird' again. After these months of friendship. After—" suddenly his face was buried in his hands— "after all these months of peace."

There was silence for a moment while Dr. Barlowe, through blurred vision, watched the bars of sunlight across a young man's hair. And noticed, for the first time, the gray in that hair. And then the voice of John Murray sounded again. He spoke, this time, without raising his head.

"I've been wrong," he said. "I admit it. Only it wasn't wickedness. It was just need. It was a momentary mistake—and I paid for that mistake with years out of my life! It isn't as if I'd ever go wrong again. There isn't a need in the world, there isn't money enough in the world, to tempt me! I'm safer," he said, his voice rising, "as an employee, as a husband, than a man who has never been tested!"

Dr. Barlowe spoke. Swiftly. Almost without meaning to. "Then why," he said, "are you afraid to tell the town of your strength? The town that has grown, so swiftly, to love you? That has grown to trust you? That will go on loving and trusting you? Why are you ashamed to tell the girl—"

But John Murray interrupted. "You're right, Doctor," he said, "in theory. Only towns don't react that way often. You're an idealist, but I'm not. I've been through it all, you see. I know. I've watched the liking go out of eyes. I've sensed the hesitancy in a handshake. Prison? It leaves a scar—a taint. It's on me, if they find it out. But if they don't find out, I'm clean—clean. Do you know what that means? To a man who's spent years in jail?"

Dr. Barlowe nodded slowly. Yes, he knew. He knew towns and the people who lived in towns. He knew what the breath of scandal, the faint thread of a rumor, could do. He knew that, in theory, possibly in practice, he was right. But he knew also (for he was an old man and understood human nature) that John Murray was right!

And yet, right or wrong, did it matter? The town's reception of a question wasn't, just now, the vital point. There was something deeper, more fundamental than that at stake. There was something more elemental.

It was a question of honesty, of truth. And for years, so very many years, Dr. Barlowe had stood for truth and honesty. His utter integrity had been, to the whole town, like a rock. The whole town trusted him. Could he betray that trust by sharing—with this young stranger to the town—a secret? A secret that might almost be called a guilty secret?

Or would the sharing of the secret justify his sense of betrayal? Would he not be right in guarding the young man's past? In letting the love of the girl, Elizabeth, know no shadow? In letting the president of the bank accept an efficient cashier at today's valuation?

But for that matter, would a life fabric resting upon a deception build toward a constructive tomorrow? Could a life woven of lies be a fine life? Or would it wither the lives all about it?

But John Murray's voice broke into his soliloquy. "Just in this moment," he said slowly, "I'm knowing what it is to be crucified. I'm watching a fine structure crumble down all around me. I'm seeing the woman I love being hurt."

So said John Murray. Nothing more. And somehow the old minister knew that the young man would no longer beg—that he had ceased to ask favors. Somehow Dr. Barlowe knew that the question was now entirely in his own hands. And the knowledge did not help. For across the knowledge lay the reflection of John Murray's hurt eyes, of his appealing smile. The sort of smile that, maybe, he wouldn't ever own again!

Suddenly Dr. Barlowe spoke. "Go back to Elizabeth, John," he said. "Leave me alone for this afternoon. I can't take your happiness in my hands and break it—for that is how you feel in the matter—all at once! Neither can I fail a whole town that has trusted me for nearly half a century. Leave me alone for the afternoon—we'll call it a truce. And I'll phone you at Elizabeth's house to tell you of my decision, as soon as I make that decision."

John Murray looked deeply into Dr. Barlowe's eyes. "I'll be waiting, sir," he said and went out, leaving Dr. Barlowe alone.

No, not alone, for all at once the minister was on his knees in the presence of One whom he had always served. And his lips, soundlessly, were asking questions.

It was almost an hour later when Dr. Barlowe rose, calmed and steadied. He saw clearly that a precious privilege was his, not a stern duty that must be met. The mistake of a foolish boy must not shatter or mar the happiness of two young people. Yes, Elizabeth must know, and the truth must come from her loved one's lips. No real happiness or peace of mind could John have with this secret hidden away from her. Always there would be the dread of her sometime finding it out. She must know, too, of the strength and courage that had urged him on when at times the odds seemed too great to overcome. He himself might have to see to *that!*

John was respected and trusted in the community and had many friends among his associates. Certainly society needed no protection from this man. After all, is it not what we are today that counts, rather than what we were yesterday?

So locked in Dr. Barlowe's heart must the secret remain, with the many others that had been brought to him by his people from all walks of life during the long years of his ministry. All other decisions must rest with John and Elizabeth alone.

And the good man smiled a tremulous smile as he reached for the telephone.

The Soul of a Violin

RUTH LEES OLSEN

Not all fathers are biological ones. It is said that, as important as books are to education and growth, they are almost always secondary to mentors, flesh-and-blood people who unsparingly give of themselves so others may grow, may become.

To the Knight of the Road, such a sacrifice seemed almost too great to ask of him.

HE was a "knight of the road." Time and space meant nothing to him, for the world was his for the asking. The starry heaven was his covering by night, the shade of waving trees his shelter by day. The vagrant breeze that cooled his cheeks whispered of bubbling brooks and fragrant orchards. He was not a tramp in the hobo sense of the word, for his name was on the honor roll of Harvard University. But he chose the open trail and the fields afar, searching for the peace and happiness his soul craved.

The sun was nearing the distant skyline when he awakened from his slumber. He sat up with his back against a mighty oak and, taking a violin from its case, drew the bow softly across the strings. A world of melody sprang forth at the touch. The birds at evening vespers paused to listen to the plaintive notes; the leaves of the trees fluttered tremulously; but the man played, lost to the sights and sounds around him. At last he raised his head, with a deep sigh of content, and looked straight into the eyes of a tall, gangling, curly-headed, barefooted boy who stood with a rapt expression on his face.

The man smiled at him in a friendly way as he questioned, "Like music?"

The boy was too absorbed in watching the instrument in the man's hands to answer, but asked a question for himself: "Say, mister, do all fiddles play like that?"

The knight of the road was plainly amused. "Well, I cannot say that they do. There is a soul in every violin, but it takes a master hand to bring forth its music. Do you play this instrument?"

The look of eagerness on the boy's face suddenly died out. "Wisht I could, but—you see, we're poor, an'—there's the mortgage. Ma says ef it wasn't for that, mebbe—someday—I can learn to play. I got a fiddle, but it don't sound no ways like yours, mister."

The man laid the violin in its case and motioned the boy to a seat on a nearby log. "Tell me all about it," he said in a sympathetic voice that made the fifteen-year-old lad long to pour out his very soul in a burst of confidence. There had been little chance in his lonely life to tell of his longings and ambitions.

He squinted at the sun and then said slowly, "It won't hurt Brindle an' Stumpie to eat awhile longer; so I guess I can visit a little spell. We don't see strangers often in this neck o' the woods." He dropped down on the log and dug his bare toes into the soft moss. "You see it's this-a-way. Ma's brother run away from home to be a sailor. An' I guess he sailed 'most all over the world. Last time he went to sea he left his iron chest with Ma an' told her to be mighty careful o' it, fer he had a treasure in it. He never did come back, an' we heard that his ship was wrecked off the coast o' Newfoundlan' in a storm. Ma felt terrible about it, fer he was her favorite brother. She wouldn't let Dad open the iron chest for the *longest* time! But one day he said ef it held a treasure, he was goin' to see it. An' he went up in the attic an' opened that chest—an' what do you think he found?"

The man smilingly shook his head. "I am sure I do not know."

There was a note of disappointment in the boy's voice. "Nothin' but some old clothes an' a fiddle. It didn't look all shiny like yours, but kinda brown and dull-like. Dad was so mad he wanted to bust it up, but Ma wouldn't let him. I promised to be awful careful with it; so I got the fiddle. There wasn't anyone to teach me how to play, but I kept on trying, an' now it talks to me 'bout the stars, an' birds, the wind an' the brook, an' a lot more things."

The knight of the road handed his violin to the boy. "Let me hear you try this."

The boy shrank back. "I couldn't play *your* fiddle, mister. It's too nice fer a farm boy. Besides, I don't know anything to play."

"Oh, that's all right," smiled the man. "Play the tunes you play when you are out in the woods alone."

The lad took the cherished instrument, oh, so carefully, and drew the bow softly across the strings. His face lighted up with joy as his fingers found their places. A cardinal trilled a few notes from a nearby bush, and catching up the song, he sent it back in exact imitation of the redbird's melody. His was a program of birdsongs, of tinkling waterfalls, and the music of wood and dell. The man listened, entranced with the woodland voices. He drew a deep breath of satisfaction as the boy finished and handed back the violin saying, "Thanks, mister. That's the best fiddle I ever touched. But ef I don't get them cows in, Dad'll fiddle me to another tune." He was away down the trail and soon lost to sight.

"A genius, and unaware of the fact," murmured the man as he watched the lad disappear. "I'll be here when the cows come lowing home tomorrow evening."

Bruce Roberts took his beloved fiddle that night after the household was asleep and stole softly out to the orchard by the brookside. He wanted to transfer the musical tinkle of the water to the bow of his violin. It was not his first visit to this secluded spot. His farm duties left him little time for music, and what knowledge he possessed had been obtained from the voices of the night. This particular evening things seemed different, for had he not listened to real music? and touched a real violin? As he drew the bow lovingly across the strings, he determined that *his own* fiddle should someday speak like that of the man he had met by the roadside.

The next evening when Bruce went after Brindle and Stumpie, he found his new friend waiting for him. "I hope you have a few moments to spare, lad, for I want to talk with you." The boy did not tell him that he had come early on purpose, hoping to hear this "wonder man" play again. Instead, he seated himself, and in answer to skillful questioning, told the simple story of his life.

He was the eldest of five children, and therefore the mainstay of his father and mother. The farm on which they lived was mortgaged, and it was all Dad could do to keep the interest up, but someday he hoped to clear it of encumbrances. His schooling privileges were limited to the winter months, but the boy, with an avidity for learning, not only led his classes, but read and absorbed every book he could borrow from the neighbors near and far. The great desire of his heart was for a musical education, but there was no possibility of his obtaining it.

A simple story, but it touched the heart of the listening man as few things had ever touched him. He possessed all this boy longed for and more. But what use was he making of his knowledge? Bruce Roberts in his place would pay off the mortgage, provide a comfortable home for his parents, and see that his brothers and sisters received a thorough education. Yes, this boy would make a good accounting of his opportunities, but how about John Williams, the knight of the road?

They sat in silence a few moments, and then the lad asked, "Are you goin' to play some more fer me, mister?"

"Perhaps," John Williams smiled, "but first I want to teach you how to handle your bow and help you about your fingering."

Bruce's face beamed. "You sure are a good man, mister! But I can't never hope to play like you. Mebbe you could write it down so's I could remember it."

Still smiling, the knight of the road took a bit of paper and a pencil from his pocket. This is what he wrote: "The spider taketh hold with her hands, and is in kings' palaces." "You are to read this every day," he said, handing it to the boy, "for it will be your guide to success."

Bruce looked at the words carefully, and as he did so, he seemed to visualize an apple tree in the orchard that he had seen but yesterday. In a notched branch of the tree a spider had built her web with painstaking care. It was supple enough to bend with the breeze, but strong enough to catch and hold even a marauding bee. Perhaps the apple tree loaded with luscious fruit was not a king's palace, but it was a good place to be.

"What do you mean, mister, by spiders and kings' palaces?" he questioned. Then John Williams explained that fame and fortune await the one who is willing to work for them.

"Do you mean that I can play my fiddle even before the President of the United States?" asked the boy incredulously.

"Yes," was the spirited reply, "and you can play before the angels of heaven, too, for I think there are times when they listen to earth's music. Now for our first lesson."

Bruce Roberts was late in bringing Brindle and Stumpie home that night, but his ears were deaf to his father's scolding. Perhaps they were still listening to the music of the stars.

For some reason incomprehensible to himself, John Williams lingered in the neighborhood for several weeks. He became acquainted with the people in the vicinity and made many friends, but it was Bruce Roberts who received the greatest benefit from his stay. Autumn breezes took the place of summer sunshine, and the nights grew sharp and frosty. School days loomed on the horizon, and the question of study became a vital one.

It was at the close of a violin lesson one afternoon that Bruce found courage to mention the thing that was nearest his heart. "Wisht you could be our teacher this year, Mr. Williams. An' you *could* ef you *would*, 'cause Dad said our old teacher sent word he had a better school and wasn't ever coming back here." Then in a burst of confidence he said, "I don't care, neither. He didn't know so much, only what he read out o' books. But I *have* to have an *education*, an'

Dad says mebbe it's too late to get another teacher." Then with a wistfulness that was pathetic he continued. "Wisht *you* would be our teacher. Dad'd room and board you, an' then we could play the fiddle 'most every night. I know Ma'd let us go in the front room, so's Dad wouldn't hear us. You *will come*, won't you?"

John Williams hesitated. Should he heed the call, it would mean giving up the free, open life of the great out-of-doors and a return to the shackles of civilization. As he waited, a voice seemed to whisper to him, "Think what your reward would be! Making men is the biggest job in the world." He glanced toward the eager boy who had pulled a much-worn bit of paper from his overalls pocket. On it were written the words "The spider taketh hold with her hands, and is in kings' palaces."

Bruce looked up. "Seems as if I'd have to know how to use my head as well as my hands! I sure do *wish* you would teach our school."

The knight of the road made no promises, but he did take up his violin and play until Bruce felt as though his heart would leap from his body for sheer ecstasy. But after his pupil had gone, the man remained under the old oak tree to fight a battle with himself. Here and now he would forever end the strife between John Williams and the call of duty to personal service for humanity.

Bruce will never forget that winter in school nor the evenings in the "front room" at the old farmhouse. A paradise of learning had opened its gates to him, and with much travail of mind and soul, he entered in and drank of the living waters of knowledge. The extra hours for study were paid for in early rising and work of hand and brain at top speed.

"Beats all what that boy accomplishes," said his father one evening after a heavy husking of corn. "He never worked like this before."

"Maybe it's the music," returned the understanding mother. "Ever since the teacher told him that brother Tom's violin was a fine instrument, he's jest lived fer that fiddle."

"Lived *with* it, you mean," replied the father. "Well, he sure does make it talk! But pshaw, what's it good fer anyway? It won't pervide his bread an' butter ner help pay off the mortgage either." Mother sighed. The mortgage was like a gray wraith, with bony fingers reaching out for every dollar that crossed the threshold of the farmhouse. It haunted her waking and sleeping hours.

Happily for Bruce, he was too much absorbed in his studies and music to worry about mortgages. But John Williams, hearing a word dropped now and then, knew that the dread of losing their home was always present with the Roberts parents. Perhaps it was the thought of making their burdens lighter, or it might have been his own love for music, that led the schoolteacher to write to the Academy of Music in a distant city for some information he desired.

Whatever the answer, he continued his correspondence with the Academy until it became a regular habit for the rural mail carrier to leave a letter with that particular return address on it at the Roberts home.

Spring, with dancing feet and flower-filled arms, came flitting over the fields and meadows. Birds nested in her hair, and gorgeous blossoms dropped from her fingers. There was a mellow softness in the air, and the brown earth called to the orb of day. The sun sent back a shower of golden beams in answer to the call, and the robins cried, "Wake up! Wake up! Spring is here."

There was a wistful longing in the eyes of Bruce Roberts as he lingered in the school yard one evening waiting for his teacher. Only a few more days of school, and then—what? He sat down on the step and tried to ease his mind by whittling on a bit of wood. "You must be trying to get something out of your system, the way you are going after that chip."

It was John Williams who spoke, and there was a twinkling smile on his face.

Bruce threw the stick aside. "Oh, I just can't bear to think of school closing now. Why, there are so *many things* I want to know! So many things to learn! Besides, there's my music—" His voice broke.

The man sat down on the step by his side. "Cheer up, lad. You've been working hard with both head and hands. Who knows but that the 'king's palace' is nearer than you dream?"

The boy shook his head. He could not trust himself with words. John Williams looked at him keenly and then rose and said, "Come on down to the old oak, Bruce. I want to hear you play that piece we composed."

Bruce went into the schoolhouse and returned with his violin. "I thought you might want me to play, and somehow today I'd rather play on my own fiddle."

John Williams nodded thoughtfully. "Just as you please, Bruce. There is no questioning the value of your violin. It is a real treasure."

A thought that had been troubling the lad's mind for some time now forced its way to the front, and he asked, "Just how much could I get fer this fiddle, if I wanted—well—say, if I wanted to sell it?" He tried to make the remark a casual one, but it was difficult to keep the voice quiver in the background.

The man refrained from looking at the boy. "Oh, I think I could get a good price for you if you decide to dispose of it. But I thought you valued your fiddle

above everything else in the world." There was no answer, and the schoolteacher knew instinctively that the boy's blue eyes were flooded with tears.

They walked down to the old familiar pasture trysting place where they had first met, and John Williams seated himself with his back against the old tree, just as he had on that evening so long ago. The curly-headed boy stood in front of him, only he was not gangling now, but straight and sturdy as the old oak itself. There was a firm set to his mouth and a light in his eyes that told of high ideals and an earnest purpose. His music, as he swung the bow across the strings, brought strange thoughts to the mind of John Williams, and once more he was a knight of the road with the world before him. Only now that world contained strange figures of the long ago. There were lilting music and eager listeners. He had thought it all dead, but—could the dead live again?

Bruce had to speak his name twice before the man brushed aside the vision. Then he pointed to the old familiar log and said, "Be seated, Bruce. I want to talk with you. School will be out Friday, and the following Tuesday I am going to the city. I want you to go with me—wait a moment—" as the boy started to speak. "I have talked with your folks, and they have consented to your going. You can take your violin with you. We will visit a friend of mine who handles musical instruments, and he will tell you what yours is worth, and what it will bring on an open market. What say you?"

Bruce pressed his beloved instrument close against

his heart until it seemed as though the soul of the one entered into the soul of the other. He wondered if this man knew just how much that fiddle meant to him. At last he gave the promise, but the joy of the journey was tinged with the bittersweet of sacrifice.

Thursday evening in the hotel lobby, John Williams turned to his boyish guest and said, "There is to be a concert at the auditorium tonight. I promised a friend of mine, who has charge of the program, that you would play your composition."

"Oh, Mr. Williams, I *couldn't* play before a lot of people. I don't know how, and besides, that's such a simple little melody! Please, *please*, excuse me!"

But John Williams had no intention of excusing him. He made an appeal that he knew the boy could not resist. "If you make good, it will mean that you can pay off the mortgage on the home and also save your beloved violin. Now I know you will play," and Bruce knew so too.

The musician had skillfully arranged so that his protégé did not stand face-to-face with the audience. At one side of the rear wall of the building hung a large oil painting of woods and hills, waterfalls and running brooks. It was so realistic that one could almost hear the birds singing in the trees. As they stood waiting their call, John Williams said, "You are not to think of the people out there in front, Bruce; you are to remember the old oak, the cardinal's song, and the laughing brook. Let your violin speak. It has a voice—a wonderful soul voice."

Bruce Roberts hardly saw the people, although subconsciously he knew they were there. There was a message in his fiddle for his well-loved friend, and once more he saw the great oak, with the knight of the road resting beneath its branches. His violin sang of strength and vital power; it was the soul of the man and the heart of the oak; then he caught the lilting notes of the cardinal and wove them in a web of trills and cadences until the audience leaned forward in breathless wonder. They heard the murmur of the little brook as it sang to the bending willows and nodding buttercups on its banks. The birds sang their evening vespers, and the katydids chirruped of the coming storm. The sky grew dark and the rumble of thunder stilled the birdsongs; the raindrops tinkled on the leaves of tree and fern. Night—darkness— wind—storm, and then a daybreak of joyous happiness: the sunrise and the awakening of the workaday world. In the finale the violin sounded a call to the palace of the King and then thrilled to the call for great endeavor and high ideals.

It was over, and the plaudits of the audience filled the great auditorium. But the boy hardly heard the applause, as he felt the pressure of his teacher's hand on his arm and heard the voice he loved say, "'The spider taketh hold with her hands, and is in kings' palaces.' You have placed your foot on the first step, Bruce lad, and I doubt not that you will reach the inner court."

They passed to the back of the stage to meet the President of the Music Association and his colleagues. Then President Lindval was speaking, and

Bruce heard him as in a dream. "We congratulate you, young man, on winning the Lindval Prize. It is not often that we hear a violin speak as yours spoke in your composition tonight. You are fortunate, not only in your conception of music, but in having for your teacher John Williams. We thought we had lost one of the greatest violinists in the country when he left us without even a farewell. We are indebted to you for his return, and we trust that he will remain with us. Here is a token of our appreciation of your efforts."

He handed the bewildered boy a slip of paper. Bruce did not know what it meant until his friend explained that it was a cash prize for his composition effort, and also that there was included a scholarship for future study at the Academy.

"And you mean they are going to *give* me violin lessons?" gasped the boy.

"Of course they are," said his friend, smiling. "And the check will go a long way toward paying off the mortgage."

"But my violin!" For Bruce could not quite comprehend yet what it all meant.

"Oh, you can keep your fiddle to practice on. It is worth a good deal now, but its value will be greatly enhanced when you have made it famous by your melodies."

There was the light of a great purpose in Bruce Roberts's eyes as he looked first at his beloved fiddle and then at his own brown hands. "'The spider taketh hold with her hands, and is in kings' palaces,'" he murmured. "Yes, *it really is true!*"

The Campus Ghost

JOSEPHINE DEFORD TERRILL

There comes a time when most of us leave home and enter that never-never land of college life. It is as much a shock to the system as leaping out of a sauna into a snowbank. Very, very few young people are prepared for it.

Most students eventually trade in their parents for mentors when they get to college. The lucky ones will find—or be found by—wise mother or father surrogates who will make seismic differences in their lives. It is not an overstatement to say that second only in impact to the parent is the impact a high school or college mentor can make in the life of a questing youth.

Such a father-surrogate was "The Campus Ghost."

Josephine DeFord Terrill wrote some of the most provocative stories I know during the first half of this century. Although known and cherished by those who read inspirational literature in those years, today she is virtually unknown. Her voice is one we can ill afford to lose.

FLORINE stood by the window of a second-floor classroom and looked out on the spring-green campus below. Dotted about the yard, like patches of flowers, were groups of brightly clad girls who, hav-ing their domestic assignments out of the way, were free for an afternoon of play. A lump of envy arose in Florine's throat—much larger than the usual one. As long as the outdoors was not particularly inviting, she could endure the long hours over her work. But when the sunshine reached long, tantalizing arms through the window, and the gay laughter from outside pene-trated the heavy walls, then a small rebellion began to foment deep inside of her. And from the depths of it, long incoherent thoughts began to form: *I'm the only girl in the dormitory who has to work all the time. Every one of the others has at least some hours to do just as she wishes!*

If only once, just today maybe, she could let her work go and run out across the springy new grass with the girls to listen to their interesting—though inconsequential—chatter! To be a part of their fun! To have no work of any sort to worry about! The lump doubled its size now that she fully understood her long-pent-up loneliness.

All the other girls in the dormitory had such pretty "work ginghams," made to wear on that day when everyone donned work clothes and went scurrying about with laundry bags, pressing cloths, and shoe cleaner. Up on her floor, they visited animatedly from room to room, pretending to have sewing or mending to do but caring little whether either was accomplished. Everyone had a feeling of homeyness, of familyness—all but Florine. Never did her week-ends begin with a prolonged stay in bed, friendly bathrobed visits, and manicure parties. Up at the usual hour, hair combed with the usual speed, dressed in the weekday skirt and blouse, she hurried off to the library, where long hours of work on books helped pay her tuition.

At lunchtime she felt like an alien in her school clothes when everyone else was in gingham or overalls, reveling delightedly in the "chory" atmosphere of the day. Her roommate—merry, irresponsible, and very popular—referred to her humorously as "the workingwoman." Florine could not have endured to be as strictly pleasure bound as was Mildred, yet there were times when she felt she would give anything for just one hour of her glorious leisure.

This afternoon as Florine left the dormitory on her way back to work, a half-dozen girls were girding shoulder packs for a five-mile hike, ostensibly in the interests of a biology assignment, though everyone knew that the birds would get little of their attention. Another group was gathering for a fudge-making at the sewing teacher's home in the village. What a world of gaiety and laughter would be stored up in their hearts when the day was over!

Florine worked always until the supper bell rang, and when she returned to the dormitory, the halls were full of girls in volleyball outfits, girls carrying wet swimming suits, girls in dusty hiking clothes: girls eager, gay, zestful, pulsating with activity and fun. Even on Sabbath she found little time to loiter about out-of-doors or share in parlor conversations. Teaching in kindergarten meant teachers' meetings; being assistant secretary of the young people's soci-ety meant strict attendance and sometimes a report to prepare. Last Thursday the first picnic of the spring had meant little to her except a chance to write the poem for the sophomore number of the school magazine. The staff had thought it good, but they hadn't known that it was the price of a whole day's fun.

Turning finally from the window, Florine went back to the desk, to the huge pile of English papers which must be corrected for Miss Wright. But she felt no zest for them today. Her heart was out on the sunny slope beneath the white ash. She forced herself to begin the first paper. It was a theme on pet dogs. "Why," she demanded crossly, "must academic juniors select such infantile subjects?" Then without another bit of warning, her face slid into the papers with a sob.

And the only reason there is a story to tell about it is because just at that very moment the door of the classroom opened and Professor Hunt stuck his head in to see who was there. Many a student has wept in the seclusion of a deserted classroom, and many a discovering teacher has slipped noiselessly away, but Professor Hunt was not that sort. He closed the door firmly behind him and came boldly down the aisle.

With a whimsical smile on his face he began to quote:

"Tears, idle tears, I know not what they mean.
Tears from the depth of some divine despair."

In shamed confusion Florine tried to laugh. But failing, she attempted an explanation. "It isn't a divine despair. It's just because I want to be lazy. Look at those girls out there on the campus having a good time. They *never* have to work. Nobody works all day long but me!" Her voice choked and she stopped.

He studied her for a moment. "Oh, I see, spring fever tears!"

"Yes, that's it, I guess," she answered, now fully in control. "I'm ashamed to be caught crying like a baby, but I, well, I get so tired of working—especially on a day like this."

"When everyone else is out enjoying the sunshine." He was smiling—but the smile was kind, and a little troubled, as if he were suddenly looking backward to years that were gone.

"Do you like to correct papers?" he asked abruptly.

"Yes, I really do."

"Better even than sitting on the campus?"

"Yes, of course, but—"

"I understand. You'd like to sit on the campus just *some* of the time. And you *should!* And yet you can't sit there all afternoon and correct papers, too, can you?"

"No," she admitted, feeling very childish.

"Why did Miss Wright give *you* the job of reading her papers?"

"Because she knows I like to, I guess."

"She didn't give it to any of those carefree little campus lizards out there in the sun, did she?"

"No."

There was a pause for a moment; then he asked, "Where do you do the poems you've written for the school magazine? Out on the campus?"

"No, up here generally."

"Up here," he repeated. "Alone." He turned as if to go. "Did you ever hear of the ghost who visited old Scrooge?"

"Why, yes, of course."

"Well, I've just had an inspiration. I'm going to play ghost and take you on a few trips. Of course, not being a real ghost, I can't make you invisible, but that won't matter. Leave your papers for a few moments and come with me."

Mystified, Florine followed Elmwood's most popular teacher out of the room, down the stairs, and out of the main building, where he paused a moment to look over the expanse of green carpet that beautified the plain brick buildings of the school. "Cast your eyes about now," he told Florine, "and see who is out here."

He led her across a strip of green and up the steps of the boys' dormitory, which they entered and rapped at the first door.

"I wonder if this young lady and I may visit Mr. Scofield?" he asked.

The preceptor nodded obligingly and took them down the hall to the last room on the court side. Everything was quiet. Only the pleasant hum from the warm outdoors could be heard. "I doubt if he's in," said the preceptor. "The sunshine has about emptied our rooms today."

"Oh, he'll be in!" Professor Hunt spoke confidently.

Sure enough, the senior's voice called a cheerful "Come!" at the rap.

"Guests to see you, Mr. Scofield," announced the preceptor.

A tall young man in shirtsleeves and a head visor opened the door. "Why, this is a pleasure, Professor Hunt! And Miss—er—Jackson! Come in!"

The ghost guide motioned Florine into the room, disregarding the preceptor's departing stare of curiosity. "We hope you won't mind our unconventional visit and our still more unconventional purpose," began Mr. Hunt. "Our sole reason for coming was to see what you are doing!"

The senior twisted his head in boyish embarrassment, and a warm Norwegian smile spread slowly over his bronzed face. "Well," he told them, "I'm just taking the afternoon off to cram some Bible verses into my head. I go into a tent effort this summer, you know, and I'm beginning to realize how little I *really* know of my Bible."

Florine gasped. Only last week he had given the sermon in the nearby city effort the ministerial band was holding, and from his ready quotations, he seemed to know the Bible almost by heart.

"You disregard the call of the great outdoors on a day like this?" reproached the professor with mock seriousness.

"Oh, it shouts particularly loud to me, but I just say, 'Get behind me!'" And his big hearty laugh filled the room. "But won't you do me the honor to sit down?"

"No thank you, John. Miss Jackson and I were wondering how busy people spend glorious afternoons like this; so we are making a few calls. Thank you for your testimony. We more clearly understand now why you are going to be a good minister someday. Good-bye."

They went out, leaving Mr. Scofield much puzzled, but still smiling.

Around the corner to the chemistry building they walked. A few boys were lolling on the grass. They passed them by and went into an inner room. There sat Norman Allen, his slim shoulders bent over a test tube.

"Time to stop, Norman. Too hot for that today," called Professor Hunt.

Norman looked up and laughed, too absorbed in the contents of the tube to even reply.

"Getting hungry?" persisted the professor.

"Why, is it lunchtime?" he asked, startled.

"The rest of us ate at twelve, but don't worry about it, Mr. Pasteur. Maybe you can stop long enough for supper."

They went out, the professor explaining that young Allen meant to be a research doctor someday. He had all the earmarks of a Walter Reed or a Frederick Banting. Every weekend he spent almost an entire day in the laboratory.

The music conservatory was next. Eva Henderson rested her fingers long enough to answer Professor Hunt's questions. Her pianoforte graduation was to be in three weeks, and she had been on the piano stool six hours already that day.

Miss Ryerson, the young vocal teacher, stopped doing trills long enough to tell them that since she gave no lessons that day, she took the time to keep her own voice from getting stale. Oh, that wasn't long: five hours singing, with rests in between! Yes, indeed, the outdoors was pounding in her veins, but she didn't want to frighten the birds away by singing out in the woods.

Up in the girls' dormitory they found Helen McPhee laboring over a talk for the next general Prayer Band program. She looked tired and warm, and Florine recalled that Helen wasn't a familiar weekend figure on the campus, as viewed from her station by the second-floor classroom window.

It was rather a shamefaced little sophomore whose steps lagged a bit behind the ghost guide as they returned to the administration building. Reaching her door, they heard a faint noise from the floor above.

"Let's see what *that* can be," suggested Professor Hunt, and they went up another flight of stairs. He opened the door of the typing room. Geraldine Daniels, seated at a small table before a typewriter, turned a weary face toward them.

"Why, Miss Daniels!" said Mr. Hunt, going toward her. "You look utterly exhausted! Surely you don't prefer pounding typewriter keys to a cool afternoon on the lawn!"

She passed a hand across her perspiring forehead. "There's nothing I'd like better," she answered dejectedly. "But I *must* practice. I am going to compete in the typing contest next month at Chicago."

"How long have you been here today?"

"I've done 30,000 words." She pointed to a heap of typewritten sheets on the table beside her.

"My dear child!" exclaimed Professor Hunt in true alarm. "Please close up that thing for the rest of the day. I'm afraid you are going to make yourself ill. Here's a young lady who will take a long walk out into the country with you."

She smiled. "Thanks, Professor Hunt. But I can't. Last year's champion did 40,000 words in one day, and I aim to do 41,000 or die in the attempt." She stood up and began to massage her aching fingers.

Florine backed her way out of the room. "I'm sorry, but I'm afraid I can't go either. I have a lot of papers to correct!"

She hurried out and ran on tiptoe down the stairs. Her heart was pounding, but her eyes were shiny when she sat down before the huge stack of work.

When her teacher again closed the door behind him, she looked up with a guilty but grateful smile.

He stood a moment looking down at her, the whimsical expression again in his eyes. "To make a truly dramatic finish the ghost should disappear without this last interview. But in case I haven't been as convincing as Scrooge's guide, I'll add the moral to our little travels this afternoon. When I was a young man, a wise minister used these words in a sermon. I'll just inscribe them on the blackboard here for you to copy."

He took up a piece of chalk and wrote: "The work that counts is that which we do when we are alone."

Florine sat there awhile, pondering the meaning of the words, and longer yet to dedicate herself to the following of them—then, very carefully, she read the first halting sentence of the theme on pet dogs.

Tenderly and Forever

AUTHOR UNKNOWN

This is an old story that I first came across more than a quarter of a century ago. Through the years, I have searched in vain for its origins and authorship.

I have read it many times to students in my classes and found by their breathless attention that the story continues to retain the same power today that it had when it was first written so many years ago.

Lovely Judith Lane will elope in two hours. To while away the time during that interminable period of waiting, she unwraps the birthday present her father had given her early that morning before he left. Her dear father, who had raised her as a single parent—alone—would, she knew, be absolutely crushed by her elopement.

The present was a book, a leather-bound book filled with handwritten pages.

JUDITH LANE put the last article into the suitcase she had been packing and snapped it shut with nervous haste. She was a lovely creature, tall and splendidly built, with straight back and long supple limbs. Her head was set firmly on a strong throat, and there was her curling hair pushed back, revealing the modeling of her fine face. But today her face was stripped of its serenity and was strained and white, for she was about to elope.

She moved to her dressing table. On it was a picture of a young man with a too-handsome face. He was dark, with bold eyes and a full-lipped, sensuous mouth. Judith knew all this—knew that her father had good reasons for disliking Harris Wilson—and yet he had gotten into her blood, had whipped her good senses to a hot passion that bewildered and frightened her and left her almost defenseless.

She took the picture from its frame, went back to the suitcase she had been packing, opened it again, and slipped the picture in. But she was not thinking of Harris Wilson now. No, she was thinking of her father—of the blow she was about to deal him. That it would be a frightful blow, one from which he would never recover, Judith did not doubt. The knowledge of this made it the bitterest moment of her life, for she loved her father. Indeed, he had been her whole world until this upsetting, unnerving romance had turned her into a creature that she hardly knew.

She sank down on the bed and stared moodily at her dressing table. If only she could rush out of the house now, at that very instant, and have no more time to think! Instead, she must wait two long, dragging hours.

Harris and she had planned everything to the dot.

It was Thursday—the maid's day out. And it was her eighteenth birthday. She was of age today. Her father had planned a birthday dinner for her at the club—for just the two of them—only there would be no celebration now. Instead, there would be a letter waiting for her father, telling him she had gone away with Harris. They would be married by the time he read the note.

How could she wait two long hours? It was agony. Her mind was filled with pictures—pictures of her life in this house with her father. This room was full of memories. She moved restlessly, and her hand touched the package her father had given her at breakfast that morning as he kissed her good-bye.

"I have something else for your birthday, Dear," he had said, "but this is your *real* present. This is a present I've been waiting eighteen years to give you."

She had been too upset all day to even open the package. Now, in her longing for distraction, she untied it idly. There was a book inside the wrappings—a book with a hand-tooled leather binding. On it was written in gold, *LETTERS TO JUDITH*.

Judith opened the book curiously and began to read.

September 10, 1921
My little girl,
This is, I am sure, your very first love letter, for you are at this moment precisely twenty-four hours old. You are lying in the Children's Hospital tucked under a pink blanket, your two small fists curled like shields against your face. I know; I have stood almost all day looking through the glass at you, wondering at the miracle of life—you are so small, so delicately perfect. I feel so unworthy, as I gaze on the intricate mingling of flesh and spirit that is you.

We came to the hospital two nights ago. Your mother was very sick. We almost lost you. But when they finally let me hold you for a moment and said you were a fine, healthy baby, I knew a happiness I had never before experienced. They tell all sorts of funny stories about fathers in maternity hospitals; as you grow up you will hear them, too. But it isn't funny—being a father for the first time. It's a soul-shattering experience. As I held you in my arms and looked into your crumpled, pink face, I wished a great many things—most of all that I had been more of a man—purer, nobler, more fitted to direct the destiny of a human soul.

You see, Darling, I am telling you my most secret thoughts—thoughts that by the time you are eighteen I will be too self-conscious to put into spoken words. If I write them down now, while my heart is so full, they will tell you all you will ever want to know about your mother's life and mine and about those first beginnings of your own existence everyone is so curious to hear about as she or he grows up. So every year I am going to write you a letter, and you will see the years unfold in these pages.

Your father

Judith let her hand fall on the written page. Her eyes were wet with tears. "Oh, Daddy," she whispered. "Daddy."

She turned eagerly to the next letter. It was dated a year later.

Dear Judith,

We called you Judith, you see. It seemed a good strong name, and if you turned out an amusing child with a turned-up nose and freckles, we could shorten it to Judy. Your mother really picked your name. She had a great-aunt she remembered as a little girl. She said she looked like a queen but always spoke so gently. I should have liked your name to be Margaret—after your mother.

How shall I tell you about your mother, Darling? I thought last year when I started to write these letters that they would be full of happy thoughts, but there are other things which you must know. Your mother is dead, Judith. She died a week after you were born.

You will have her pictures. In fact, I have a great many pictures of her for you—snapshots I like best because she looks so alive and natural in them. There is even a painting of her by Loreux. But only I can paint your real mother for you—or show you even a little of what you have lost in losing her. She was very beautiful to look at. Perhaps you will look like her. You do now, somewhat. You are already a tall child, and your eyes are well-shaped, long and heavy-lidded, and, too, of that heavenly dark blue that is so rare. She had white skin that had a kind of opalescent glow to it like mother-of-pearl and a beauty that no painter, even Loreux, could catch.

But it was not any of these things that made me love her so. I would have loved her if she had been homely and dowdy, for she would still have been herself. She was a complex character, but perhaps the trait I loved best in her was her courage. She was afraid of nothing, least of all of life. She met life with open arms. When she knew you were coming, her only thought was of delight. I never once heard her express the slightest fear that she might die or that anything might go wrong. When she was suffering so terribly the night you were born, she never complained. Every time I looked in on her she held out her hand to me and smiled until she was too weak to lift her hand. And then she simply smiled.

A week later I went home one night thinking all was as it should be. I had hardly gotten in the house when they sent for me . . . she was dying. I don't remember how I reached the hospital, her room, her bed. She opened her eyes and looked at me—a long look—revealing everything she had not strength to say.

Carry on, it said. This is life; this is the chance we took. I couldn't have loved you more if I lived forever.

I knelt down beside the bed and took her in my arms. She was almost gone, and yet she spoke one sentence: "Love her for me, too. . . ."

What a strange thing death is! The separation between it and life is so complete, and yet a moment before it happens the loved one speaks—speaks in character—as if that broken sentence were only a part of conversation. Then came silence—immutable, endless . . . "Love her for me, too. . . ."

How can I love you as she would have done? I've tried this year; I'll go on trying. But no matter what I do, it won't be enough. You took your first staggering steps into my arms; I sat beside your crib all night when you had the croup—I held you in my arms against all rules of experts—before the fire in winter months and out in the garden your mother made as spring came on . . . but nothing that I can do will be enough. Your mother is dead.

Judith read on and on. She forgot the time. She read about when she was two, three, and four. All her little naughtinesses and the smart things she said; her small, loving ways. Then she was five. She went to kindergarten. And something more tremendous threatened to happen.

Judith Dear,

You are five now. Almost . . . well, not almost . . . you are a little girl now. You have soft, lovely brown hair that curls about your neck. You go to school. I took you myself the first day. And I said to myself, like any foolish mother, "I haven't a baby anymore. My baby is grown up."

Something else has happened this last year; I must tell you about it. I have met someone—a woman—of whom I have grown very fond. I won't say I am in love. I could never love anyone as I loved your mother. But this girl is companionable. Her name is Kate Dexter. I met her at a dinner party given by some friends, and I liked her. She sat next to me at dinner. We found lots to talk about—books we both had read, etc. We finally got around, as is inevitable with people who hit it off, to life and its problems—love, marriage, and children—and I told her about you. I'm afraid I gushed about your virtues, because she laughed and said, "Here, now, you're making her sound like a dreadful little prig."

That brought me up short. I knew I was being a bore, but I didn't even resent that crack at me. There seems something frank about a person who would say a thing like that.

Would you mind, Judith, I wonder, if I married again? I've been terribly lonely sometimes. I'm the sort of fellow who needs a wife. I like to putter around the house, dig in the garden, drag out the hose, and water the lawn.

That's the sort of man who needs a wife. The nightclub variety can find companionship anywhere, and they don't mind if it's a different face for every night of the week, but I like stability in life. I like to have a few people in for dinner, play games—go on vacations with my wife and child . . . I could never go in for one of those backstreet romances . . . yet, I do need a woman in my life. Would you mind, Dear? Kate Dexter has a quick, alert mind and a kind of worldliness that I think might be good for both of us. I think you need a woman's love and tenderness, too.

You are asleep now. I've just run up to have a look at you. I wanted to wake you—you looked so unearthly— wake you and ask you the question: "Shall I marry Kate Dexter?" I feel the need of reassurance, and you are the only other person most concerned.

A year later.

Judith,

I couldn't do it. I couldn't marry anyone. It was a fool's paradise that I lived for a couple of months, and I am back to sanity now—have been for a long time.

A day or so after I wrote my last letter to you—that is

a year ago—I asked Kate Dexter to our house for dinner. I made a great event of it. You had on a little white dress. It had no sleeves—some blue business on the shoulders—and your arms were so soft and white, like a baby swan's wings. You came into the living room and gave Kate your hand and bobbed a curtsy, the way you had been taught. Kate gave her hand to you, and then she looked into your solemn face and laughed.

"You're your daddy's girl, aren't you?" she said. "He looks at me sometimes just the way you're doing. It makes me feel as if my soul were in full view for all to see and understand."

All during dinner you kept your eyes fixed upon her as if you had some childish standard of measurement you were judging her by. I felt as nervous as a wet hen; I wanted you two to like each other so. Then you went off to bed, and Kate and I walked in the garden for a while.

There was nothing reminiscent of my Margaret in Kate that night. I had taken her out in the garden to propose to her, but I couldn't do it there. There was the faint, sweet smell of stock in the air, and Kate seemed oblivious of it all. She stepped on a blossom as her foot slipped on the path. The flower broke off and lay inert. I picked it up.

"I've gotten mud all over my shoes," she said lightly, but there was an undercurrent of annoyance in her voice.

"Let's go for a ride," I suggested. "It's getting cold out here."

But when I was leaving her that night at her door, she said, "Could I borrow Judith some afternoon, Dick?

I think I could get better acquainted with her if I had her to myself for a few hours."

I agreed. "Yes, of course." She knew what had been on my mind.

Kate lives in a pretty little house out at Lakeview. People wondered why a young, single woman wanted to live alone out in the country, but that was one of the things I liked about her. It shows stamina when a person can depend on herself for companionship. I feel that lack in myself.

Finally the afternoon came. Maria dressed you in your best and smartest—not a foolish father's idea of how a little girl should look. Kate called for you. I was at the office, but I phoned home to find out if you had gotten off and if all was well.

If they hit it off today, I'll ask Kate to marry me tonight, I decided.

The idea took such possession of me that I decided to quit for the day, run out to Lakeview, and surprise you both—perhaps take you home and then carry Kate off to dinner and a proposal.

As I drove up to Kate's house, there was no one about. I thought it a little odd when no one answered the bell. So I walked around the house to the back door. In the kitchen was Elsie, Kate's maid, her head on the table; she was sound asleep.

She sat up abruptly. A frightened look flashed on her face. "I musta dozed off," she explained.

"Where are Miss Kate and my Judith?"

"Oh!" cried Elsie and ran out of the house down toward the river. I ran after her as fast as my feet could carry me.

You were sitting on the small dock by yourself, your feet hanging over the edge, a stick with a string and a pin fastened to it clutched in your hands. When I saw that you were safe, I slowed up.

"And Miss Kate—where is she?" My voice was stern.

"She'll be back—she thought to be back before five. She didn't expect you, sir."

I didn't doubt that. "Where is she?"

"It was some party she didn't expect that came up. She's never one to stay home from a party. You won't tell her that I fell asleep, will you?"

"No, I won't tell her that."

I took you by the hand and started for the car. As we got to it, Kate swept up the driveway. Her face looked as crestfallen as so skillfully controlled a face can look. Then she tried to cover it with bravado.

"Dick, this is a surprise! I just ran over to Olcott—brought home some things for dinner. I was going to ring you up." She pouted a little. "Now you've spoiled my surprise."

So that was the end of my romance. I found out later—what seemed to be the worst aspect of the whole thing—that Kate had told you not to tell Daddy she had gone off for the afternoon. She had made up some cock-and-bull story and thrown a bribe or two in by way of good measure. I think I'll never be tempted again. Not that I have any prejudice against second marriages, but I just didn't have the courage to take the chance with you. *"Love her for me, too."* I just couldn't take that chance.

Judith read eagerly on. The years slipped away beneath her fingers. She was sixteen.

My Darling,

You are sixteen tonight, and you have gone to a party—with a boy; I managed to drive you over. It was a feat of the most offhanded, subtle diplomacy. At twelve I am going back to get you and your cavalier.

Your cavalier only turned into a cavalier tonight. Up to that moment he was the kid from next door—Prof. Thorpe's boy I like so much who wore a dirty sweatshirt. Tonight he, too, blossomed. He called for you in his tuxedo. Thorpe can't afford such extravagances, but he did. Then you came down. You had on your first long dress. It was white—white net, I think they call it. You wore a flower tucked into your hair. I wanted to cry. You were like a dream of youth walking into my living room—so fragile, so untouched. I was almost afraid to speak, to touch you, for fear you would vanish.

Then young Thorpe said, "Christmas, you can't walk over to Kenwood's in that getup!"

Your face fell.

"I'm going to give you a lift," I said on an inspiration. "It's on my way to the club. I'll call for you on the way back, if you want me to."

"Oh, could you, Daddy? Then Jimmy can put the price of the taxi toward our tennis court. We're paying for it together, you know."

Oh, my little girl, how can I shield you from life and yet let you live it to the full? I'm almost forty-five—I never was as brave as your mother. I feel that the more of life I live, the less courageous I am for you.

I want you to have everything you should—love, a home of your own, children—yet how can a girl have wisdom of choice—how—when it has taken me a lifetime to learn the ways of the world? You will say, "But Mother and you . . ." And I will have no answer except that it was a happy Providence and hope that the same Power may watch over my child.

Judith,

You have fallen in love with the wrong man. When you were sixteen I wrote you a letter—in it I prayed that the very thing that has happened would not happen. But it has.

I could not keep you to myself. I couldn't say, "Don't do that." I had to let you live a normal girlhood—ride, swim, learn to drive a car, handle a boat, ski. Through every danger you met and accepted, I met and escaped a hundred times. I had to let you meet all kinds of people. You had to develop some power of discrimination for yourself. Yet somewhere along the line I must have fallen.

Tonight as I sit here writing this last letter to you, I have gone back over the years and tried to see where I failed. But I don't know. Perhaps after all, I should have married Kate Dexter. She would have given you hard, worldly wisdom that would have been a better shield than what your sentimental old father has tried to arm you with. You have been Diana to me—cool, aloof, virginal. I am all bewildered at seeing a thick-handed, hot-eyed stranger turn you into Venus—languorous and heavy limbed.

Oh, my darling, what is it? What has happened to you? Can't you see that this Harris Wilson is not your sort—that in a few years you will grow to hate him, hate the sound of that impudent voice with its easy cajolery and cheap wit? I know it is not really you who has fallen in love with him—not my Judith. It is as if your body were apart from your soul. You are young and strong, full of vitality. He has kissed you. I've seen it in your face when you've come in from being with him. That greedy mouth on your fresh, sweet lips—it makes me sick all over.

It isn't love, Judith! It isn't love! I know. My darling, it isn't love. Love is something that can be cool as fresh water. It can strengthen, not weaken; elevate, not debase.

Good night, my darling. God guard you and keep you from harm. Remember that, no matter what you do, I shall love you tenderly and forever.

Your father

Judith flung herself face downward on her bed and burst into stormy crying. Not since she had been a little girl had she cried like that.

"Oh, Daddy!" she sobbed over and over.

He had meant to show her her life. Instead, he had shown her *his*—the long, quiet years of self-sacrifice, dull years, watching a small girl grow up. All the high adventure that might have been his he had exchanged for the privilege of guiding her stumbling feet, taking her hand close in his along the way. *This* was love.

Slowly, Judith sat up. She unlocked her suitcase again, pulled out the picture of Harris Wilson . . . and tore it into a million pieces. She walked over to the dressing table and dropped the pieces into the wastebasket.

"No, Harris," she said. "You might be good enough for me. I'm not as good as my father thinks I am." Then she smiled—a woman's smile—as if the girl Judith had indeed come of age. "But if there should ever be a little Judith, Harris—you'd certainly not be good enough for her!"

A Lesson in Forgiveness

T. MORRIS LONGSTRETH

Here they were at dawn: a sleepy-eyed boy who had run away from home, and a President who was struggling under a terrible responsibility.

Little did either know that this chance meeting would change so many lives.

T. Morris Longstreth, born only thirty-one years after the terrible Civil War had bled to its close, grew up listening to the veterans tell its tales. Although Longstreth wrote many books during his long and illustrious career, today it is for this poignant story that he is remembered.

THE Ripley brothers were as different in nearly every way as are the rapids and still pools of a mountain stream. Perhaps that is why they loved each other in a way not usually meant by "brotherly love."

Will Ripley was the "still pool." He was thoughtful to the point of appearing drowsy, honest as daylight, mild-tempered, and twenty. He was up north in Pennsylvania somewhere, either alive or dead, for the date of this story is July 7, 1863, which means, as you can read in the dispatches of the time, that the terrible Battle of Gettysburg was just over. The Ripleys, on their farm near Washington, had not heard from him for some time.

Although Will was no soldier at heart, he had responded to Lincoln's call for more men two years before, leaving his young brother, Dan, at home to help his father and mother. Dan was now fourteen, a high-strung, impetuous, outspoken lad of quick actions and hasty decisions. He was the "laughing rapid." But for all his hastiness, he had a head and a heart that could be appealed to—usually.

The only thing to which he could not reconcile himself was the separation from Will. Even Will's weekly letters—which had seldom missed coming until recently and which always sent messages of love to Dan, coupled with encouragement to stay on the farm as the best way to aid the cause—scarcely kept him from running away and hunting up his brother. Dan knew that he and his collie, Jack, were needed to look after the sheep; he knew that his father, who was little more than an invalid, must have help. But to see the soldiers marching set him wild to be off with them. In fact, Jack seemed to be the anchor which held him. Dan sometimes even thought that he loved Jack next to Will.

The summer of '63 had been unbearably hot. There had been an increasingly ominous list of military disasters. Even the loyal were beginning to murmur against Lincoln's management of the war. Then Will's letters had ceased, and Mr. Ripley could get no satisfaction from headquarters.

Dan was irritable with fatigue and his secret worry; his family were nearly sick with the heat and the tension.

The climax to this state came from an unforeseen event. Jack, crazed either by the heat or by some secret taste for blood, ran amuck one night, stampeded the sheep, and did grievous damage. Farmer Ripley doubtless acted on what he considered the most merciful course by having Jack done away with and buried before Dan got back from an errand to the city. But to Dan it seemed, in the first agony of his broken heart, an unforgivable thing. Weariness, worry, and now this knife-sharp woe changed the boy into a heartsick being who flung himself on the fresh mound behind the barn and stayed there the whole day despite the entreaties of his mother and the commands of his father.

That evening his mother carried some food out to him. He did not touch it; he would not talk to her.

Some time later as the night wore on, he stole into the house, tied up some clothes into a bundle, took the food at hand, and crept from his home. Once more he went to the grave of his slain pal. What he said there, aloud but quietly, need not be told. Sufficient it is to know that a burning resentment toward his father filled him, coupled with a sickening longing to be with his brother Will. Ill with his hasty anger, he thought that Will was the only one in the world who loved or understood him.

In the wee hours of morning he left the farm, forever as he thought, and turned down the road which led to the Soldiers' Home, not far away, where he hoped to find someone who could tell him how to get to Will's regiment. The sultry, starless heat of a Washington midsummer enclosed him; the wood was very dark and breathless; his head throbbed. But he pushed on, high tempered, unforgiving; he would show them all!

Suddenly he remembered that he had not said the Lord's Prayer that night. Dan had been reared strictly. He tried saying it, walking. But that seemed sacrilegious. He knelt in the dark and tried. But when he got to "as we forgive our debtors," he stopped, for he was an honest lad. This new gulf of mental distress was too much for him; it brought the tears. There in the dark by the roadside, Dan lay and bitterly cried himself into an exhausted sleep.

At the same hour another worn person, a tall, lean-faced man with eyes full of unspeakable sorrow, was pacing the chamber of the White House in the nearby city. The rebellion had reached its flood tide at Gettysburg three days before. The President had stayed the flood, bearing in tireless sympathy the weight of countless responsibilities. Now, all day long, decisions of affairs had been borne down upon him—decisions that concerned not only armies but races; not only races but principles of human welfare. He was grief stricken still from his son Willie's death, and his secretary in the room downstairs, listening unconsciously to the steady march of steps overhead, read into them the pulse beats of human progress. Lincoln had given instructions that no one was to interrupt him. He was having one of his great heart battles.

Finally, shortly before dawn, the footsteps stopped, the secretary's door opened, and the gaunt, gray face looked in. "Stoddard, do you want anything more from me tonight?"

The secretary rose. "I want you to go to bed, sir. Mrs. Lincoln should not have gone away; you are not fair with her or us."

"Don't reproach me, Stoddard," said Lincoln kindly; "it had to be settled, and with God's help, it has been. Now I can sleep. But I must have a breath of air first. There's nothing?"

"Only the matter of those deserters, sir, and that can wait."

The President passed his hands over his deep-lined face. "Only!" he murmured. "Only! How wicked this war is! It leads us to consider lives by the dozen, by the bale, wholesale. How many in this batch, Stoddard?"

The secretary turned some papers. "Twenty-four, sir. You remember the interview with General Scanlon yesterday."

Lincoln hesitated, saying, "Twenty-four! Yes, I remember. Scanlon said that lenience to the few was injustice to the many. He is right, too." Lincoln held out his hand for the papers, then drew it back and looked up at Stoddard. "I can't decide," he said in a low voice, "not now. Stoddard, you see a weak man. But I want to thresh this out a little longer. I must walk. These cases are killing me; I must get out."

"Let me call an attendant, Mr. Lincoln."

"They're all asleep. No, I'll take my chances with God. If anybody wants to kill me, he will do it. You must go to bed, Stoddard."

The two men, each concerned for the other, shook hands in good night, and Lincoln slipped out into the dark, his long legs bearing him rapidly northward. During the heat he usually slept at the Soldiers' Home, being escorted thither by cavalry with sabers drawn. But he hated the noise of it and during Mrs. Lincoln's absence was playing truant to her rules. When he neared the home, he felt slightly refreshed and turned into a wood road. The sky to his right began to lighten.

By the time dawn showed the ruts in the road, Lincoln realized that he was tired. "Abe, Abe," he said half aloud, "they tell me you used to be great at splitting rails, and now a five-mile stroll before breakfast—well! What have we here?"

The exclamation was occasioned by his nearly stepping on a lone youngster lying in the road. The boy raised his head from a small bundle of clothes. The tall man stooped with tenderness, saying, "Hello, Sonny. So you got old Mother Earth to make your bed for you! How's the mattress?"

Dan sat up and rubbed his eyes. "What are you doin'?" he asked.

"I appear to be waking you and making a bad job of it," said Lincoln.

"You didn't come to take me, then," exclaimed Dan, greatly relieved. "I wouldn't 'a' gone!" he added defiantly.

Lincoln looked at him sharply, his interest aroused by the trace of tears in the boy's eyes and the bravado in his voice. "There's a misunderstanding here," said Lincoln, "almost as bad a misunderstanding as Mamie and her mother had over Mr. Riggs, who was the undertaker back home." Here the gaunt man gave a preliminary chuckle. "Ever hear that story, Sonny?"

Dan shook his head, wondering how such a homely man could sound so likable. Lincoln seated himself on a fallen tree trunk. "Well, it was this way—" And he told the story.

Dan's quick, impetuous laugh might have disturbed the early-rising birds. Lincoln joined in, and for an instant Dan completely forgot dead Jack and his deserted home. For the same fleet instant Lincoln forgot his troubles in Dan's laugh. The boy chuckled again. "I'll have to tell that to Fa—" He didn't finish the word, remembering with a pang that he was not going to see his father again.

Lincoln caught the swift change on his face, and it was his turn to wonder. He knew better than to ask questions. You can't fish for a boy's heart with question marks, neat little fishhooks though they be. So he said, "Our sitting here when we ought to be getting back home reminds me of another story."

"Tell me," said Dan, well won already to this man, despite the gray, lined cheeks and the sadness that colored his voice. Dan didn't know yet who he was. He had not seen the cartoons that flooded the country during the election. He was too young to go in alone to the inauguration, and the idea of the President of the United States sitting with him in the woods was too preposterous to cross his mind.

When Dan had laughed heartily over the second story, Lincoln said, "Well, Sonny, I reckon we ought to be moving, don't you?" He helped the lad with his bundle.

"Are you going to the war, too?" asked Dan. "I am."

"You!" exclaimed Lincoln. "Why, you're no bigger than my own Tadpole, and he's only a wriggler yet. Does your father know?"

"I reckon he does by now," said the boy darkly. "Father's an early riser. You see, he killed my dog without my knowin', and so I left without *his* knowin'."

The hardness of the boy's voice hurt Lincoln, who said, "What's your father's name, Sonny?"

"William Ripley—that is, senior. Will, that's junior, my brother, is off at the war. I'm Dan. I'm going to find my brother. I don't care if I never come back. I loved Jack better than—than—" His voice choked.

Lincoln put his hand on the boy's shoulder. He was getting the situation. "Jack was your dog?" asked the big man as gently as a mother.

"Yeh. And Father shouldn't 'a' killed him unbeknownst to me. I'll never forgive him that, never!"

"Quite right," said the wise man, walking with

him. "Don't you ever forgive him, Dan. Or don't ever forget it—under one condition."

"What's that?" asked the boy, a trifle puzzled at the unexpected compliance of his elder with his own unforgiving mood.

"Why, that you also never forget all the kind and just things that your father has done for you. Why did he kill the dog, Dan?"

"Well—he—killed—some sheep," said the boy. He would be honest with this tall, gentle, and grave person who understood so readily.

"How old are you, Dan?"

"Fourteen, going on fifteen."

"That's quite a heap," said Lincoln musingly, "quite a heap! In fourteen years a father can pile up a lot of good deeds. But I suppose he's done a lot of mean ones to cancel 'em off, has he?"

"No," admitted Dan.

His frankness pleased the President. "I congratulate you, Dan. You're honest. I want to be honest with you and tell you a story that isn't funny, for we're both in the same boat, as I size up this proposition—yes, both in the same boat. I am in the Army, in a way. At least, I'm called commander in chief, and occasionally they let me meddle in a little with things."

"Honest?" said Dan, opening his eyes very wide. He had been so absorbed in his own disasters that he had accepted this strange, friendly acquaintance without question. But now, although the forefront of his consciousness was very active with the conversation, the misty background was trying to make him compare this man with a certain picture in the big family album with another one pasted on the dining room cupboard door, the same loose-hung person, only this one had a living rawness—maybe it was bigness—about him that the pictures didn't give, like a tree, perhaps. But it *couldn't be* the President talking to him, Dan. If it was, what would the folks at home—and again his thought stopped. There were to be no more "folks at home" for him.

"Honestly, Dan. But sometimes they don't like it when I do meddle. There's a case on now. Last night I pretty nearly had twenty-four men shot."

"Whew!"

"But I hadn't quite decided, and that's the reason I came out here in God's own woods. And I'm glad I came, for you've helped me decide."

"I have!" said Dan, astonished. "To shoot them?"

"No! Not to. You showed me the case in a new light. Here you are, deserting home, deserting your father, bringing sorrow to him and to your mother, who have sorrowed enough with Will in danger and all; you're punishing your father because he did one deed that he couldn't very well help, just as if he'd been a mean man all his life. And it's like that with my twenty-four deserters, Dan, very much like that. They've served for years, faithfully. Then can any one thing they do be so gross, so enormously bad, as to blot out all the rest, including probably a lifetime of decent living? I think not. Is a man to blame for having a pair of legs that play coward once? I think not, Dan. I tell you what I'll do, Sonny." The tall man

stopped in the road, a new light shining in his cavernous, sad eyes. "I'll make a bargain with you. If you'll go home and forgive your father, I'll go home and forgive my twenty-four deserters. Is that a bargain?"

The boy had been shaken, but it was difficult to change all at once. "It is hard to forgive," he murmured.

"Someday you'll find it hard not to," said the great man, putting out his huge palm for the boy to shake. "Isn't that a pretty good bargain, Dan? By going home, by ceasing to be a deserter yourself, you will save the lives of twenty-four men. Won't you be merciful? God will remember and perhaps forgive you some trespass sometime even as you forgive now."

Something of last night's horror when he could not say that prayer, and something of the melting gentleness of the new friend before him touched the boy. He took Lincoln's hand, saying, "All right. That's a go."

"Yes, a go home." Lincoln smiled. "I suppose I'll have to turn now."

"Where's your home?" asked the boy, knowing, yet wishing to hear the truth, to be very sure; for now he *could* tell the folks at home.

"The White House," replied Lincoln. "But I wish I were going back to the farm with you."

The boy heard him vaguely; his jaw was sagging. "Then you—are the President?"

Lincoln nodded, enjoying the boy's wonder. "And your servant, don't forget," added Lincoln. "You have been a help to me in a hard hour, Dan. Generals or no generals, I'll spare those men. Anytime I can do anything for you, drop in, now that you know where to find me."

The boy was still speechless with his assured elation.

"But you'd better—wait." And Lincoln began hunting through his pockets. "You'd better let me give you a latchkey. The man at the door's a stubborn fellow, for the folks will bother him. Here—"

And finding a card and a stub of a pencil, he wrote:

Please admit Dan'l Ripley on demand.

A. Lincoln

"How's that?"

"Thank you," said Dan proudly. "I reckon I should 'a' guessed it was you, but those stories you told kind o' put me off."

"That's sometimes why I tell them." And Lincoln smiled again. "It's not a bad morning's work—twenty-four lives saved before breakfast, Dan. You and I ought to be able to eat a comfortable meal. Good-bye, Sonny."

And so they parted. The man strode back the way he had come; the boy stood looking, looking, and then swiftly wheeled and sped. He had been talking to the President, to Abraham Lincoln, and hearing such talk as he never had heard before; but especially the words "You have been a help to me in a hard hour, Dan"—those words trod a regular path in his brain. He ran, eager to get to the very home he had been so eager to leave. Forgiveness was in his heart, but chiefly there was a warm pride. He had been praised by Abraham Lincoln! Of this day he would talk to the end of his days. Dan did not know that the major part of the day, the greatest in his life, was still to come. Certainly the dawning of it had been very beautiful.

Breathless and with eyes bright in anticipation of telling his tale, he leaped the fences, ran up to the back door, and plunged into the house. The kitchen was quiet. A misgiving ran over him. Were they all out in search of him? Would he have to postpone his triumph?

In the dining room a half-eaten meal was cooling. He explored on and, coming out to the spacious front of the house, found them—found them in an inexplicable group around a uniformed officer. Tears were streaming down his mother's cheeks. His father, still pale from his accident, looked ashen and shriveled. They turned at Dan's approach. He expected that this scene of anguish would turn to smiles upon his arrival. He was amazed to find that his return gave them the merest flurry of relief and alleviated their sorrow not at all.

"Danny dear, where have you been?" asked his mother.

"The Lord must have sent you home in answer to our prayers," said his father.

Then they turned back to the officer, pleading, both talking at once, weeping. Dan felt hurt. Did his return, his forgiveness, mean so little to them? He might as well have gone on. Then he caught the officer's words: "Colonel Scott can do no more, madam. The President cannot see him, and more pardons are not to be hoped for."

Mrs. Ripley turned and threw her arm across Dan's shoulders. "Danny—Danny—you are our only son now. Will was—" She broke down completely.

"Will was found asleep while on duty, Dan, and—"

"Is to be shot?" asked the boy. "I wonder if he was one of the twenty-four." They looked at him, not understanding.

"The Lord has restored you to us. If we could only pray in sufficient faith, He could restore Will," said Farmer Ripley devoutly. "Dear, let us go in and pray. We should release this gentleman to his duty. We can talk to the Father about it."

Dan realized with a sudden clearness that his brother, his beloved, was to be taken from him as Jack had been taken. It shook his brain dizzy for a moment; but he knew that he must hold onto his wits—must think. There was Abraham Lincoln, *his friend!*

"You pray," he cried to his father shrilly, "and I'll run."

"Run where, Dear? Will is in Pennsylvania."

"To the White House, Mother. He said, 'Anytime I can do anything for you, drop in.' *Anything,* Mother. Surely he'll—"

"Who?" cried both his parents.

"Why, the President, Mr. Lincoln!"

"But the President is busy, Dear."

"He'll see me—I know he will!" said Dan. "Look! We have a secret together, the President and I have."

And the boy showed his card and poured out his story.

The mother saw a break in her gray heaven, saw the bright blue of hope.

"We must go at once," she said. "Father, you are not able to come with us, but pray here for us."

"Please take my horse and carriage," said the officer.

"Yes," said Dan, "let's hurry. Oh, I'm glad, I'm so glad!" And the joy at his lucky turning back shone in his face as he helped his mother into the vehicle.

"May God help you!" said the officer.

"He does," said the boy, thinking.

It was high noon when the doorkeeper of the White House, hardened into a very stony guard by the daily onslaught of Lincoln seekers, saw an impetuous youth leap from a light carriage and help a woman up the portico steps toward him.

"In which room is the President?" asked Dan.

"He's very busy," said the doorkeeper, probably for the five hundredth time that morning. "Have you an appointment?"

"No, but he said I should drop in when I wanted to, and what's more, here's my latchkey." Dan, trembling a little with haste and pride, showed him the card "A. Lincoln" had written.

The man looked quizzically at it and at him. "In that case," he said dryly, "you'd better step into the waiting room here."

There must have been forty or fifty people crowded into the anteroom, each on some urgent errand. Some were in uniform; all looked tired, impatient, important. Dan saw the situation and knew that Lincoln could never see them all. He whispered to his mother and showed her to a chair, then went up to the doorboy and asked if the President was in the next room. The boy admitted the fact, but would not admit anything further, including Dan. The annoyed looks on the faces of the waiting people deepened. "Does this urchin [said their looks] expect to see the President today, when so many more important persons [such as we] are kept waiting?"

Dan, not caring for etiquette when his brother might be shot at any moment, slipped under the arm of the doorboy and bolted into the room.

Lincoln was standing by the window. He looked around in surprise at the noise of Dan Ripley's entry. He recognized his walking partner, made a motion for the doorboy, who had one irate hand on Dan, to withdraw, and said, "Why, Dan, I'm glad to see you so soon again. You're just in time to back me up. Let me introduce you to General Scanlon."

Dan looked into the amazed and angry eyes of a Union general who, practically ignoring the boy, went on to say: "Mr. President, I repeat that unless these men are made an example of, the Army itself may be in danger. Mercy to these twenty-four means cruelty to near a million."

The President, worn not only from his sleepless night but from the incessant strain of things, looked grave, for the general spoke truth. Lincoln turned to Dan. "Did you go home, Sonny?"

Dan nodded.

"Then I shall keep my half of the bargain. General, this boy and I each walked the woods half the night carrying similar troubles, trying to decide whether it was best to forgive. We decided that it was best, as the Bible says, even to seventy times seven. Dan, how did your folks take it?"

Dan spoke quickly. "It would 'a' killed them if I'd run off for good, for they just got word that my brother Will—you know I told you about him—is to be shot for sleeping on watch. I just know he was tired out—he didn't go to sleep on purpose. I told my mother that you wouldn't let him be shot, if you knew."

Lincoln groaned audibly and turned away to the window for a moment. The general snorted.

"I brought my mother in to see you, too," said Dan, "seeing as she wouldn't quite believe what I said about our agreement."

Lincoln looked at the boy, and his sunken eyes glistened. "I agreed for twenty-four lives," he said. "But I don't mind throwing in an extra one for you, Dan."

And this time the general groaned.

"Stoddard," added the President, "will you see if there is a Will Ripley on file?"

The secretary left the room. Lincoln turned abruptly to the general. "You have heard me," he said. "I, with the help of God and this boy, threshed out the matter to a conclusion, and we only waste time to discuss it further. If I pardon these deserters, it surely becomes a better investment for the United States than if I had them shot—twenty-four live fighters in the ranks instead of that many corpses underground. There are too many weeping widows now. Don't ask me to add to that number, *for I won't do it!*"

It was rare that Lincoln was so stirred. There was a strange silence. Then the secretary entered with, "Yes, sir, a Will Ripley is to be executed tomorrow for sleeping on duty. The case was buried in the files; it should have been brought to you earlier."

"Better for the case to be buried than the boy," said the President. "Give me the paper, Stoddard."

"Then you will!" said Dan, trembling with joy.

"I don't believe that shooting the boy will do him any good," said Lincoln as the pen traced the letters of his name beneath this message: "Will Ripley is not to be shot until further orders from me."

Dan looked at it. "Oh, thank you!" he said. "Can I bring Mother in to see it—and to see you?" he asked.

The President looked down into the shining face and could not refuse. In a moment Dan's mother was in the room. She was all confused; the general was red with irritation.

She read the message. It didn't seem quite clear to her. "Is that a pardon? Does that mean that he won't be shot at all?"

"My dear madam," replied Lincoln kindly, "evidently you are not acquainted with me. If your son never looks on death till orders come from me to shoot him, he will live to be a great deal older than anyone else."

She stretched out both her hands, crying, "I want to thank you, sir. Oh, thank you, thank you!"

"Thank Dan here," said Lincoln. "If he had not let the warmth of forgiveness soften his heart, Will Ripley would have died. And perhaps, if I had not met him in the woods at dawn, I might have gone into eternity with the blood of these twenty-four men on my hands. Dan helped me.

"True, they are erring soldiers, Mrs. Ripley. But we must consider what they have done and what they will do, as intently as we consider the wrong of the moment. Good-bye, Dan; we shall both remember today with easy consciences."

The waiting crowd in the anteroom could not understand, of course, why that intruder of a boy who had fairly dragged the woman in to see the President so unceremoniously should bring her out on his arm with such conscious pride. They could not understand why the tears were rolling down her cheeks at the same time that a smile glorified her face. They did not see that the boy was walking on air, on light. But the dullest of them could see that he was radiant with a great happiness.

And if they could have looked past him and pierced the door of the inner room with their wondering glances, they would have seen a reflection of Dan's joy still shining on the somber, deep-lined face of the man who had again indulged himself in—mercy.

At Home

WINIFRED KIRKLAND

Getting old. None of us is ever ready for it. None of us really wishes to reverse roles with a parent—perhaps because such an act reminds us that we are next in line for such a humiliating shift.

Marcia Elman had reversed roles with her father, and in so doing, she had accelerated his decline.

Now . . . she wondered . . .

Winifred Kirkland (1872–1943) is little known today. Early in this century, however, besides her short stories, she wrote books such as Polly Pot's Parish, Christmas Bishop, Portrait of a Carpenter, *and* Star in the East. *This story hails from an earlier era, a time when it was expected that—as soon as one's house was in decent shape after moving to a new community— the neighbors would be invited to an "at home."*

AT HOME, of course, he was just Father. To the big world he was Professor Richard Elman, author of various historical works, full of life and energy and kindling thought. Those books were, however, perhaps a little in the past, as was Professor Elman himself.

Marcia Elman was a young woman who, when she had a thing to do, did it. There came a day when something had to be done about Father, and Marcia did it; she moved Father and the books and the household goods five hundred miles, from Hartleigh to Brewster. Of course they missed Hartleigh, missed the old college town, missed the house on the hill, Professor Elman's home during all his professorship, the house where all his six children had been born. Five of them had gone out to their own places in the world; but Marcia, the youngest, at sixteen had remained to be her father's housekeeper and homemaker. That was nine years ago.

The uprooting had aged Father more than ever, but what else was there to do? Suppose they had stayed on in Hartleigh; despite his growing remoteness and absentmindedness, could Father have failed to perceive that he was becoming something of an old story in Hartleigh? An occasional pilgrim still climbed to the house on the hill, but Hartleigh itself climbed less and less often.

Clearly, it was better to come to Brewster, which had no academic traditions. It was a pleasant spot. Marcia congratulated herself on her choice of the new town and on the new house, which had a study where her father could be comfortably out of the way of visitors.

There had been a great many visitors, cordial, welcoming people, who inquired politely but a little haltingly about the great professor and his books, as if they were embarrassed at not being better informed. About Marcia's own books, Brewster showed itself frankly and fully appreciative—much to the girl's astonishment. Not until she met this flattering welcome did she realize the fame of her three little historical romances, which in truth were careful and charming. In Hartleigh, where people had known her as a little girl, she was not used to having anyone except her father appreciate her little volumes—but here in Brewster, appreciation and hospitality due to it were so cordial that Marcia was growing to feel an almost painful responsibility about living up to it.

She had not been prepared to find in remote little Brewster people like Miss Peek, as fragile and exquisite as the priceless china on her heirloom shelves; like Dr. Copley, the great oculist, who had made a discriminating collection of Etruscan curiosities; like Mrs. Holman, who was at once the charming leader of Brewster society and an authority on musical biography. Marcia accepted invitations to one house after another and carefully made her father's excuses for remaining away. You would not have thought that Marcia Elman feared anything, but she was mortally afraid of the day when she would have to entertain Brewster.

She and her father had moved in June, but the autumn found Marcia still postponing the "at home" she had resolved upon. The change had not benefited her father. His broad, thin shoulders were more stooping than ever. Once he had had an unerring sense of direction, but now Marcia feared to let him walk without her. She kept an anxious hand at his elbow always, for once in a while he stumbled. In this companionship Marcia was the better able to protect her father against strangers, whose polite greeting he returned vaguely, but whom he seemed shy of meeting.

The day came when Marcia was ready for her at home. The rooms stood wide and welcoming and beautiful with Marcia's arrangement of autumn leaves. Everything had been done; in the dining room the candles stood ready to light, the coffee urn ready to bubble. Marcia herself, although she had personally supervised every preparation, was dressed before any of her assistants and had come rustling down the stairs. Everything had been done but one thing—nothing had been done about Father! Out from somewhere Father came, shuffling, hesitant, and anxious.

"Marcia," he said, "you have forgotten the study. There are no leaves decorating the study. Is it too late for us to fix up something now?"

"Father, I knew you wouldn't want to meet so many people. The study is so far away that nobody will bother you. I don't want to have anyone—at my party—disturb you!"

Marcia was standing in her soft white dress, bending her stately, black-crowned head above a bowl of yellow chrysanthemums. She could not see her father's face as he looked at her, but she raised her head, startled by an odd ring in his words: "I can do nothing to help you, then, Marcia?"

"No, Father dear, nothing. And you may feel perfectly safe—I'm sure no one will discover the study."

He went away. Marcia looked at the broad, stooping

shoulders, the uncertain feet, the drooping, silvered head. Her eyes grew blind a moment.

"Oh, if they could only have seen him as he used to be—Dr. Copley and Mrs. Holman and Miss Peek and all of them! It used to be Father that people came to see, but now people want to come to see me, and I've somehow got to live up to it! Oh dear, I wonder whether anyone will come!"

Whereupon Marcia flung high her head and did live up to it! For Brewster came and came, until the wide rooms hummed and a bobbing mass of heads moved about Marcia as she stood, white-gowned, black-haired, and stately.

A few guests inquired in a polite, perfunctory way about her father; nearly all talked of the pleasure that Marcia's books had given them. Everything seemed to be going well, but gradually the crowd thinned away, although Marcia had said good-bye to no one. There was only a little group in the dining room, but a cheerful ring of voices came from down the hall. Marcia passed round the staircase—someone had discovered the study!

It was a spacious study, which was fortunate, for everyone in Brewster had crowded into it, and at the same time everyone was struggling to give Professor Elman a little room in front of the fireplace. He was standing with his back to the fire and his audience in front of him. His handsome head was flung back, and the thick silver hair was tossed from his high brow. He was speaking, and across his lips quivered the old marvelous smile. His eyes were shining with a youthful radiance. It was Father as he used to be!

Marcia stole unobserved from the doorway. She stood silent and pale. Could it last, this restoration? Was it in anyone's power to make it last? What could they have been talking about, she wondered, to make her Father look like that?

When the company surged back upon Marcia to take their farewell, she learned what they had been talking about. It seemed hours before the last guest departed, hours before Marcia could go to the study to see whether Father was still there, Father as he used to be. He was standing by the mantelpiece still, and the radiance had not left his face.

"My famous daughter!" he said, and behold, the radiance on his face was all for Marcia!

"Listen to what Brewster said to me about you!" he exclaimed. "Somebody said to me, 'Miss Elman's *Portrait Painter* makes Sir Joshua Reynolds and his circle so real to me that I feel, as I listen to their conversation, as if I were an eavesdropper and ought to cough or sneeze to warn them of my presence.'

"And somebody else said, 'I never liked fact and fiction mixed until I read Miss Elman's books.'

"And somebody else said, 'We know that we are provincial in Brewster, and that there are a great many Brewsters in the world, but I do not believe there is one home where Miss Elman's books are not read.'

"There, that is what Brewster thinks of my daughter! So you see, your at home has been successful, Marcia!"

"*My* at home! Oh, no, Father, *your* at home! I understand Brewster at last. It was not I they were after. I am thankful I don't have to live up to that any longer. They wanted *you*. You had hidden yourself away, but they wouldn't go until they found you. Listen now to what Brewster said to *me* about *you*. Somebody said, 'We were getting to be afraid your father's health would never be equal to the strain of meeting us. It is good to find him so wonderfully young!'

"And somebody else said, 'We were not afraid to meet you, but we were afraid that you, after meeting us, thought we were not fit to meet your father.'

"And somebody else said, 'How kind your father has been to us! So great a man might easily have felt himself above us!'

"There, that is what Brewster thinks of my father!"

Young, strong, glowing, she stood looking at him; but even as she looked, the light faded from his face and left it wistful and questioning.

"But is that what Marcia thinks of her father?" he asked. And suddenly Marcia knew that it lay within her power to keep the radiance upon his face or to banish it forever.

"*I*, Father! I! Don't you know that I have always thought you the most wonderful person in the world?"

"But do you think that now, Marcia, now that I am old?"

"Father, who ever said that you are old?"

"Nobody ever said so, but Hartleigh thought so, and Marcia thought so, and I have come to think so, too."

"Father!" she faltered. "Oh, Father!"

"Did I behave all right, Marcia?" he asked. "I was staying close in the study, as you told me to. I did not want to disturb anyone at your party. It was not my fault, Marcia, that somebody discovered the study."

But at the thought of that discovery and the invasion that had followed, he could not help smiling. "They are kind people here, but funny and naive, not much like Hartleigh. I'm not quite sure about the names, but it was your Miss Peek, I think, who said to me, 'I wonder how Hartleigh ever let you come to us!' And a Mrs. Holman said, 'It is so wonderful to have a really great man come to Brew-ster!' And Dr. Copley, a remarkable man, by the way, said, 'Your books have been almost a religion with us here always. Our respect for them makes us almost afraid to mention them.' And he besought me, so humbly, to examine his Etruscan collection. He lives on South Street, the fifth house beyond the trolley line, the house with a small purple spot on the lowest step. You see, I'm still able to find my way about and notice things."

His eyes twinkled at Marcia, but hers were wet.

"Oh, Father, of course you're not old! And you're never going to be, if I can help it!" She came and stood within her father's arms.

"Oh, Father," she whispered, "I feel as if I were a little girl again, and you had come back from somewhere!"

"Isn't it perhaps you yourself, Marcia," he asked gently, "who has come back?"

Are You Going to Help Me?

MARK VICTOR HANSEN

Fatherhood. It is more than merely being there, more than just paying the bills, more than giving wise advice, more than being a friend or mentor, equal even to unconditional love, in fact, as supremely important as that is.

Fatherhood can be summed up in one word: dependability. Simply put, it means that one can be depended on, no matter what. That one's word represents a Gibraltar of strength upon which to build a life.

Mark V. Hansen, coauthor of that surprise best-seller of 1994, Chicken Soup for the Soul, *details in that book just such a father.*

IN 1989 an 8.2 earthquake almost flattened Armenia, killing over thirty thousand people in less than four minutes.

In the midst of utter devastation and chaos, a father left his wife securely at home and rushed to the school where his son was supposed to be, only to discover that the building was as flat as a pancake.

After the traumatic initial shock, he remembered the promise he had made to his son: "No matter what, I'll always be there for you!" And tears began to fill his eyes. As he looked at the pile of debris that once was the school, it looked hopeless, but he kept remembering his commitment to his son.

He began to concentrate on where he walked his son to class at school each morning. Remembering his son's classroom would be in the back right corner of the building, he rushed there and started digging through the rubble.

As he was digging, other forlorn parents arrived, clutching their hearts, saying, "My son!" "My daughter!" Other well-meaning parents tried to pull him off of what was left of the school saying:

"It's too late!"

"They're dead!"

"You can't help!"

"Go home!"

"Come on, face reality; there's nothing you can do!"

"You're just going to make things worse!"

To each parent he responded with one line: "Are you going to help me now?" And then he proceeded to dig for his son, stone by stone.

The fire chief showed up and tried to pull him off of the school's debris saying, "Fires are breaking out; explosions are happening everywhere. You're in danger. We'll take care of it. Go home." To which this

loving, caring Armenian father asked, "Are you going to help me now?"

The police came and said, "You're angry, distraught, and it's over. You're endangering others. Go home. We'll handle it!" To which he replied, "Are you going to help me now?" No one helped.

Courageously he proceeded alone because he needed to know for himself: "Is my boy alive or is he dead?"

He dug for eight hours . . . twelve hours . . . twenty-four hours . . . thirty-six hours . . . then, in the thirty-eighth hour, he pulled back a boulder and heard his son's voice. He screamed his son's name, *"Armand!"*

He heard back, "Dad?! It's me, Dad! I told the other kids not to worry. I told 'em that if you were alive, you'd save me and when you saved me, they'd be saved. You promised, 'No matter what, I'll always be there for you!' You did it, Dad!"

"What's going on in there? How is it?" the father asked.

"There are fourteen of us left out of thirty-three, Dad. We're scared, hungry, thirsty, and thankful you're here. When the building collapsed, it made a wedge, like a triangle, and it saved us."

"Come on out, boy!"

"No, Dad! Let the other kids out first, 'cause I know you'll get me! No matter what, I know you'll be there for me!"

Dodsworth's Beans

VINCENT G. PERRY

Five boys had good reason—nay, excellent reason!—to leave Brixton; five boys wrote their fathers asking permission to transfer to Redway. And they gave reasons.

Cal Taggart's father said yes—so he left.

Buddy Talbot's parents sent permission—so he left.

Dick Dodds's father told him he could leave.

Harry Cousins's father arrived on campus to personally escort him to Redway.

That left Jack Branton. His father agreed, only if conditions were met. TOUGH conditions . . . for Father never pampered.

THERE they stood in a massive pile—hundreds upon hundreds of empty tins in which once had been safely packed millions of Dodsworth's Beans. Discarded monuments to enormous appetites these, for every bean that had reposed in those tins had been eaten by the boys and staff of the Brixton School.

"Look here, fellows," Jack Branton told his companions as he indicated with one sweep of his arm the direction in which the pile lay, "look and weep.

Beans—Dodsworth's Beans! The trademark of Brixton School!"

From four husky voices came forth four long drawn-out groans.

"In all the world are there so many beans eaten as we eat here?" Jack demanded. "Why do we stand it—why don't we strike or something?"

"Yes, why don't we?" echoed the four voices; and then as an afterthought, one voice, Harry Cousins's, added, "But what would be the use? Professor has a way of breaking up strikes—"

"And remember the half-holiday strikes," came mournfully from Dick Dodds.

Yes, every boy remembered those two strikes and their disastrous endings. Another strike would find no sympathy in that school, not even a strike against what they felt to be the greatest indignity of all, Dodsworth's Beans.

The boys did have a grievance, there was no doubt of that. As Jack Branton put it, it was a question if in any one place besides Brixton there were so many beans eaten. Dodsworth's made up a good part of almost every meal; certainly never a day passed but that they were served once at least.

The trouble probably began when Dr. Brixton, owner and headmaster of the school, had served in the Army. He saw there, no doubt, what a great food beans were and came back with the firm impression which he worked out to extreme. And now, after a whole term of bean eating, these five chums gathered together in an indignation meeting.

This was on a day after nine straight meals of beans and with very little else which satisfies schoolboy appetites. Then to cap it all, Jack Branton had a letter that day from his cousin at the Redway School in a town twenty-five miles away. Jack alone knew the contents of that letter, but now he brought it forth.

"I've just got to read it to you, boys," he told the others, "this one paragraph about the meals, anyway. Listen: 'Wonderful eats we have here, Jack—just as good as at home, and you know what that means. Yesterday we had big baked potatoes with a slab of butter melted inside each one, scalloped corn, and a lot of other things, with pumpkin pie an inch thick to top it off. Today we sat down to the best stew and dumplings I ever ate, and the dessert was homemade ice cream. Tomorrow we'll probably have—'"

"Stop! Stop, I implore thee!" interrupted Buddy Talbot, who was noted for his huge appetite.

"Do you think it is true, or is your cousin just fooling?" Cal Taggart asked.

"My cousin's a reliable chap," Jack told them, "and lots of schools give good eats—why shouldn't they, with the prices they charge; and every headmaster isn't as partial to beans as Dr. Brixton."

"Well, it doesn't matter what he gets—we get beans!" Jack declared. "And how are we going to stop it?"

There were many suggestions, but finally it was decided that the best course—and certainly the safest and wisest—was to write home a complaint and ask to be sent to another school. The rates at Brixton were no lower than at Redway, and their parents could have no object in keeping them where the meals were so unsatisfactory, the boys reasoned.

That night five letters were posted to five different fathers, and in each was a most urgent request for a removal from the school. Redway, of course, was their preference.

Jack Branton took longer than the others to write his letter. He knew his father always wanted facts—and he gave them to him. In detail he went into a description of the meals; in fluent language he described the agonies of a constant bean diet—and he wound up with a strong appeal that he felt would move the heart of any parent, even a hard businessman like his father. He read the letter over with a feeling of pride. It was certainly a letter his father would not be ashamed of, and it had the one thing his father liked—force.

For three days the five boys waited without one answer to their letters—then Cal Taggart got his letter. He was to leave for Redway School. Arrangements had been made over the telephone for him, and the headmaster at Brixton had been notified of the withdrawal.

With a happy heart Cal packed up and left. The other four boys parted with him merrily. "We'll be with you before the month is out," they told him; and he went away believing they would.

Next day Buddy Talbot was summoned to the office. Dr. Brixton had instructions from his parents to release him that day and send him bag and baggage to Redway School. Buddy left the office the happiest boy in the whole school and was soon on his way.

Four days passed, and the three boys who remained began to feel uneasy. Monday's mail, however, set their minds at rest. In it was a letter from Dick Dodds's father instructing him to prepare to leave at the end of the week. That left Jack Branton and Harry Cousins still to hear from home.

On Friday just before Dick was ready to depart, a big car drove up to Brixton School. Harry Cousins spied it from a window and gave a whoop of delight. It was his father's car, and his father was driving. Mr. Cousins had come for a purpose. There was a lengthy interview in Dr. Brixton's office, and then Harry came to announce to the waiting pair that his father was taking him that evening to Redway School, and that Dick Dodds could go along with them if he cared to.

"It's too bad you haven't your letter, old-timer," they said to Jack as young Branton went out to the car to see them off, "but you'll be with us before long."

"Sure I will." Jack tried to look happy, but somehow he couldn't. With the departure of the last of his chums, a great foreboding had come to him. Why didn't his dad write—why was he always last? What if he couldn't go to Redway with the others?

And then he cheered up. The letter with the desired permission would surely be there in the morning!

But it wasn't—nor in the other mornings that followed—and poor Jack was beside himself with worry. He had never hated beans half so much as he believed he hated them now.

At last the boy despaired. His father had ignored his letter, that was all—and it hurt.

It was different with Jack's dad than with any of the

others, for though Jack worshiped him with all the ardor of his young heart, there had always been a gap between those two that hadn't got them very close together. Perhaps that was because his mother had died when he was a little fellow and the father had been away from his boy a great deal.

But he had not neglected to answer his son's letter. The truth of the matter was that he had been away on a very important business trip, a trip from which he returned without having accomplished what he set out to do.

For weeks the merchandising, the copy, and the art departments of Branton Advertising Agency, of which he was president, had worked on a series of advertisements and an advertising campaign plan for a prospective client—a client that planned to spend many thousands of dollars in advertising. The agency was anxious to secure the business of this firm, and Mr. Branton himself had gone to close the deal. But he was faced with failure.

"Your copy is high class, all right, but it's not what we want," the head of this firm told Mr. Branton. "We want something different—something so different that it will attract worldwide attention, and we'll give our business to the advertising people who produce something like that for us."

That firm was Dodsworth and Company, makers of Dodsworth's Beans.

Immediately upon his return to his office, Mr. Branton got into action. He summoned the heads of the copy department, the art department, and the merchandising department in private conference and told them in most emphatic terms what was expected of them.

"You've simply got to get something new for Dodsworth's Beans," he declared.

The conference over, he turned to his mail. His secretary had opened all his letters save those marked personal, and Jack's was on top of those. Branton pushed everything else aside as he opened his son's letter. He liked to hear from his boy—he was secretly very proud of him, though he never let Jack suspect. As he read Jack's letter, Mr. Branton's face grew serious; now he paused in deep thought. After he had finished the letter, he read it again, and then as he pushed it aside he chuckled merrily.

"We are not the only ones having trouble over Dodsworth's Beans." He smiled to himself—and then he was struck with an inspiration.

"Miss Collins," he called to his secretary, "I want you to take a letter to my boy."

Jack had given up all hope when the letter arrived. He caught sight of the envelope which bore his father's business address, then hurriedly stole away to his study so that he might be alone to receive the word he had waited for so long. Was he to go to Redway or stay at Brixton? He was not long kept in doubt.

The letter began "Dear Son," and went on:

I've been doing some thinking about this problem of yours, and it has brought one of my own to mind. You have a grievance against Dodsworth's Beans; well, so have I. Just at present this whole organization is working on the hope of getting something entirely new in advertising for the Dodsworth people.

You must know a lot about those beans—seeing that they're your main diet. Why not show us what you are made of and write some advertising for them? If the ads you write sell, you can go to Redway School. Otherwise you can remain along on Brixton meals, and I just can't see that it wouldn't be pampering you to let you change over. You know I never pamper. But if you can write some advertising or think up an idea, then you will have earned the right to choose another school. How's that?

Dig in, young man. Write as forceful advertising as you do a letter to your dad, and you'll be a valuable member of this firm someday.

Jack finished it and quickly sank into his chair dumbfounded. This was the very last thing he had expected. Permission to leave for Redway or flat refusal was all he had looked for—but this—it left him speechless.

At first, indignation filled his heart, for he felt his father's ultimatum was too severe, and it looked as if his dad were laughing at him. The more he thought of it, however, the better he felt about it. After all, there was a chance to show his dad what he could do—show him that the boy was growing into a man and could do things. There was a lot of the enterpris-

ing spirit of the father in the son, and it was this spirit that came to Jack's rescue now.

"I will write him some ads on Dodsworth's Beans," Jack declared, "and they'll be ads he can sell."

For more than a week Jack just tried thinking up ideas. It was on the campus during field day that he got his big inspiration. Right around him were boys of wonderful physique and great athletic ability— why not write them into ads?

From that day on Jack was busy in every hour but those devoted to study—and even during those hours he had his mind on his advertisements as much as his books. Every sunny afternoon he was out with his camera.

Ned Brooks, the crack shot-putter of the school, was the first of Jack's camera studies. He got an excellent snap of Ned with the shot held high over his head. As soon as the picture was developed and printed, Jack attached it to the advertisement he had written about Ned. He got three excellent water snaps of Roy Cairn, the champion sculler; one snap of Larry Campbell, the long-distance swimmer; another of Fred Perkins, the sprinter. Then he went in for prop pictures—got one of the baseball team, the basketball team, the football team, every other team in the school, too. He had an advertisement for every picture, an advertisement crediting the great skill and prowess of each athlete and each team to the constant eating of Dodsworth's Beans. Into each advertisement he tried to work realism, punch, and a bit of humor.

But when the series was all written and the snapshots attached, Jack felt as if something were lacking. Each ad was separate. What he needed, he thought, was one ad to link up the whole series. Then came the thought of an interview with Dr. Brixton on the important subject—beans. Jack didn't dare a real interview, but sat down and wrote an imaginary one. He had heard too many of the doctor's speeches on the great food value of beans not to know what to put in that interview, and when it was finished, it was a masterpiece of memory if nothing else, for Jack had quoted the doctor almost as he had spoken on so many occasions. To this advertisement Jack attached a clipping picture of Dr. Brixton.

It was on Monday when Jack got his work together and ready to mail to his father. With it he wrote a letter saying the snapshots were to illustrate the copy.

When J. C. Branton came down to his office on Wednesday morning, the package from Jack was waiting for him. He opened it with a feeling of curiosity, though he hadn't much hope of finding anything there of value. He had imposed this task on Jack more in a spirit of fun than anything, and he had wanted to test the boy, too.

However, as he read the first advertisement, he was delighted—the second was every bit as good, and right down through the series they seemed to get better.

"The boy has done it!" Branton cried as he jumped to his feet. "Here are ads that will get the Dodsworth people!"

Quickly he called his copy chief, and they went over the advertisements together.

"Great!" was the verdict.

The art department required a week to get the rough sketches prepared from the snapshots Jack had sent. But just nine days after Jack's copy had left Brixton School, J. C. Branton, the chief of his copy department, and the head of his art department took a trip to the home city of Dodsworth's Beans.

"Marvelous, gentlemen," declared their advertising man when he had examined the series. "Just what we've been looking for—something unique, entirely different from any ads that have ever appeared on canned goods. Let me congratulate you, Mr. Branton. Your organization is indeed a live one."

The day the final word of approval came from Dodsworth's, Mr. Branton decided on a business trip to Europe. That's why Jack received a wire that read: "Dodsworth people accept your advertisements. Pack up for home at once. You leave with me next week for a three months' trip to Europe. After that, Redway School is yours. Dad."

The three months' trip stretched out to four months, for the father liked the process of getting acquainted with his son for the first time.

When Jack did arrive at Redway School, he was greeted enthusiastically by his cousin and with no less spirit by his chums who had preceded him from Brixton.

"Now, Jack, for a real Redway meal," his cousin exclaimed as the dinner hour approached.

The boys were all seated when a great covered silver dish was brought in and placed at the head of the table. From under it was issuing most tempting looking puffs of steam. Jack was not near enough to get a whiff of the aroma, but he drew in his breath just the same.

Following grace, the master at the head of the table rose, put his hand on the handle of the cover, and then before he lifted it, began:

"Boys, I have a surprise for you. We masters have been discussing the matter of food for some time. It has been thought that perhaps our food here is a little too rich for young, growing boys. This has been brought to our attention most forcibly lately by a series of rather remarkable advertisements run by the makers of a well-known brand of beans. You have all seen these ads. They have been in almost every paper everywhere. A great deal of publicity has been given our rival school Brixton, for it seems the boys at Brixton and the masters there are of the belief that those beans are responsible for their great athletic prowess and general good health. Which may be so. At any rate, we are not at all opposed to taking an example from a rival—so now, on each Wednesday for dinner we will serve Dodsworth's Beans."

And Jack sighed.

Dad Walters' Son

LOUISE GENTRY

One son had already let Dad Walters down. But now—just when it seemed there might be another to take his place, disillusion struck again.

Had his life really been in vain?

OLD Dad Walters straightened himself slowly and painfully and looked down at the drowsing valley of the Tucannon. The sun was shining, and behind the old corrals cool, thick masses of cottonwoods and willows blotted the slow-moving shimmer of the creek. Beyond were the rough, sagebrush-studded hills, stretching away into the north and south until in the distance, merging with the eastern range, they sealed in the silent valley. The shadow of an eagle flying high over the cliffs above him drifted past, a grotesque blot of black on the sunlit expanse of the canyon wall, and even at this distance point he caught the sweet scents that floated with the wind from out of the blossoming orchard tracts.

As the old man stood there, stiffly erect, staring out at the ranch on which he had spent his whole life, he drew a short, sharp breath that was almost a sob.

His sunken eyes burned with longing, and his parted lips trembled as if to cry.

"I guess I'm pretty much of a failure, all right," he muttered brokenly.

It was strange that after so many years he should catch himself listening for the voices of the herders calling to their collies; it was strange that as each evening crept by, he continued to miss the bleating of armies of sheep bedding down in the corrals beyond the barns.

"Maybe I'm just getting old and childish, but I don't know—I don't know—" He shook his head dully as he turned about to gather up his tools.

Halting every few feet to rest or to gather a few of the brilliant Indian paintbrushes growing beside the trail, the old man labored on down the slope. As he went, he tried to convince himself that with only one band of sheep, he would not need the old reservoir, but even as he argued with himself, he visualized the broad ditch stretching away from the spring-filled basin in the canyon. He saw again the masses of showy flowers that had bloomed along its banks twenty years ago. Sarah had always been so proud of her flowers.

"Maybe if I could have fixed the thing again, she would have been coming outside more and getting a little stronger during the nice weather," he reproached himself as he crossed the porch and opened the kitchen door.

Crushing the bright blossoms which he held out to her, Sarah smiled at the old man tenderly.

"Pretty things, aren't they, Dad?"

After fumbling about in the cupboard, she brought out a familiar, squatty black vase, crowded the flaming flowers into it, and patted them into place with tremulous old hands.

Sitting by the fireside later in the evening, she still gazed upon them as Dad opened the day's paper. She was thinking of the summers, now long past, in which Chester, her only son, had brought home handfuls of those vivid blossoms; she was remembering the day that she stood beneath the great box elder on the lawn, watching Dad drive away, with Chester sitting up very stiff and straight beside him. Again she saw her boy frantically waving a last, long farewell as he was carried out of sight around the bend of the road.

When they were gone, Sarah had turned back again to the rooms that seemed so empty, with her hand pressed hard against her breast and her lips quivering as if with sharp pain.

"He's gone," she said, and then again, "he's gone."

She stumbled to the door and looked long at the knoll that had stolen him from sight. Then quickly she turned and went upstairs, shutting her door behind her. When Dad came back, she heard him crossing the parlor and came down to him with her face weary and tear-stained, but filled with the peace of victory and a glory that was not of the earth.

More than once in the days that followed, Sarah set the table for three, forgetting that only Dad would come.

"Dad, where's—" she would begin and then stop abruptly.

"What, Mother?"

"Oh, nothing." But her eyes, straying off the plate behind the table, told him what she had thought to ask.

Fully twenty years had passed away since then.

"Well, Mother." Dad was smiling at the sweet, gentle-faced old woman tenderly. "It seems to me that we are both getting pretty drowsylike tonight, and since I'll have to make a trip to town tomorrow, maybe we had better be getting to bed now."

Dad returned just after nightfall the next day. Sarah, busy with baking, did not know that he had come until, hearing footsteps on the porch, she looked up in time to see him poking his head through the half-open doorway.

"Got that extra plate on today, Mother dear?" he asked, smiling his own genial smile.

"Why, Dad—"

But Dad was already facing the other way. "Come on, step right into the kitchen here, Son." As he spoke he flung wide the door.

Uttering a half-choked cry, the old woman rushed forward with her arms outstretched in welcome. Then gasping pitiably, she shrank back, with a little moan breaking from her lips, for the young man who stepped forward all unsuspectingly to meet that welcome was not her son.

"Now, Mother," Dad explained soothingly, "it's just our new hired man, Grant Hardesty. I found him there in town, and I thought maybe he could help me a bit around here. I've decided to open the old reservoir."

Still gasping, Sarah looked up at the stranger who was standing just inside the kitchen door, twisting his cap awkwardly about in his hands. For a long moment she stared at him. It was not, however, the hopelessly crippled back that caught and held her attention, but the white face, the compressed lips, and the large brown eyes which dwarfed the thin, pallid face on which weeks of unspeakable anguish had left their clear imprint. The nose was well formed, and the face, if it had not been so thin and drawn, might have been called handsome.

In sudden confusion she found herself stammering out an explanation: "I—I thought for a moment that

Dad meant that our boy was coming back and—but come right on in, Mr.—?"

"Just Grant, Mother, just Grant," Dad said quickly.

Sarah's glance searched the boy's face, and what she saw there sent her to her knees before the oven to attend to her baking, surprised to find her eyes full of tears.

"Dad," she said, "run along into the parlor while Grant washes up a bit before supper. There's water here on the stove, soap on the table, and plenty of clean towels there on the rack. You go ahead and help yourself. I'll have to be tending these rolls".

When she rose and stole a glance at Grant, he was standing with his back to her, combing his hair before the cracked mirror beside the kitchen door. Soon, however, he turned around and smiled at the dainty, frail old lady by the stove.

The next morning Sarah brought out her best tablecloth and placed the vase of flowers in the center of the table. There was also a plate of the fat, brown cookies of which Chester had always been so fond. Sarah impatiently awaited the men's coming.

"I wonder if he'll like the cookies? I put in some extra nuts and raisins this time," she murmured as she fluttered about over her cooking.

Grant did not disappoint her; he walked straight over to the table and filled his hands.

"Um, these are delicious," he exclaimed, turning to face Sarah. "I know you baked them just for me. Now didn't you?"

After supper that night, Dad Walters read the paper as usual, but Sarah did not become drowsy as she listened to his droning voice, for Dad soon threw the paper aside.

"Sing, boy?" he asked, turning to his new hired man. Sarah somehow hoped that he would.

"A little."

"Well then, Mother, let's all sing some good old song together before we go to bed. What shall it be?"

Hobbling off to the bookcase and drawing out a brown leather volume, she found that which she sought, after turning a few pages. She hesitated just a moment, then suddenly put the book in her husband's lap. Dad Walters' face flushed. He started to hand the book back, and then, as if ashamed of his action, passed it on to Grant.

"There, can you sing that for us, Son? That's the one we sang so much when Chester was here. It seemed as if I would never want to hear it again, after Chester decided that he did not wish to carry on the old Walters' sheep business, but I do now. Can you play the organ, Son?"

*"There were ninety and nine that safely lay
In the shelter of the fold,
But one was out on the hills away
Far off from the gates of gold."*

The singer halted, and the two who looked up at him in surprise saw that his face was very white.

Again came the refrain. With uplifted head and with his eyes looking far away, he sang on:

"Out in the desert He heard its cry,
Sick and helpless and ready to die."

Dad and Mother Walters neither spoke nor moved. They could not. That clear, sweet voice held them spellbound and made their hearts ache with longing for something, they knew not what. The clear, full-toned notes filled the air and hovered over them until, caught in the spell of that aching voice, Sarah threw back her head, the raptness of her face telling that she, too, was hearing the triumphant cry of the Shepherd. Dad Walters unconsciously bent forward with his face in the shadow of his hand, for he had suddenly quite lost his grip.

Grant finished, and as the last note died away into silence, he rose and looked down at them as if surprised that they should weep. Abruptly, then, he turned and left the room.

After that night, Grant somehow took the place of their own son to the two old people. Dad Walters once more took an interest in making his ranch the best in the valley. One night he spoke to Sarah of his new plan.

"Sarah, when this year is over, I am going to adopt Grant and deed this ranch over to him."

"Oh, Dad!" Sarah cried, and her eyes glowed with happiness, for much as she had missed her boy, it had hurt her more to see Dad discouraged.

It was three months later that Sarah waited in growing alarm for the men to come in to supper. The hands of the clock dragged themselves around the face of the dial until at last, when she thought that she could not stand it a moment longer, there was a movement on the kitchen porch, and someone was coming toward the door.

"Supper has been ready a long while, Dad. Why have—" Sarah took a step closer to him and, looking up into his face, asked in a choked whisper, "Grant? Where is he?"

Dad put out his hands and stumbled forward.

"He's gone," he said brokenly.

"Gone?" echoed Sarah.

"Yes, Mother." The old man's voice shook. "I sent him to look for the cows. They came in by themselves right after he left, but he's gone."

"Why, Dad, he'll be back in a little while."

But Dad Walters was not comforted. "No, he won't ever come back. I can't report him, Mother! He's like a son to me. I can't report him."

"Why, Dad—"

Slowly Dad Walters lifted a haggard face to meet his wife's questioning gaze. "I found him over there in jail, and I liked him somehow, so I took him out to work for me for board and room. I promised to report if he tried to get away or anything; but I never thought he would. He wasn't really bad, just never had anyone really to care, and then he got in with the wrong sort of companions. I've got to give him a chance to get away, Mother. I'll tell the sheriff after a day or two, but I can't tonight."

"You promised, Dad?" Sarah asked sadly. "I love him, too, but—" She paused, looking steadily into his face.

Suddenly the old man turned to her, and putting out both his hands blindly, burst forth, his voice coming in dry sobs: "Oh, I will. I will. I love Grant, too, and there isn't anything that I wouldn't do to help him, but I will go, and no one will ever know—how much—" Dad was unable to proceed. Rising, he passed out into the night, and Sarah, left alone, buried her face in her hands.

It was a little after midnight that a car halted on the canyon road. Now and then a rock tumbled down the hillside as some object far up the slope moved about.

"Who's there?"

There was silence for a moment and then a faint voice called back, "It is I, Grant Hardesty, sir. I fell over the cliff here and hurt my back." The voice broke, but in a moment it was heard again. "I'm working for Dad Walters, sir. Would you help me get there, mister?"

So it was that the deputy sheriff brought the boy home, fainting with pain and exhaustion. All night long a doctor and the two white-faced old folks watched over him until at dawn he stirred and opened his eyes.

"I couldn't find them," he said faintly. "I was away off there on the top of the ridge and it was dark. I slipped and fell."

His eyes closed, and they thought he had fainted again. "I was afraid I'd die up there, and that you'd think I fell and was killed while I was trying to get away."

At this point Grant's voice suddenly broke, and he lay for a few moments silent, his face working while he struggled with himself. And then all at once he grew calm and, lifting his eyes, looked out of the window at the glowing sunrise. "I prayed that someone would come along that old hill road. I fainted then, but when I came to, I saw a light down there on the road and heard someone call out to me. I don't deserve your love. I was in jail because—"

"Stop!" cried the old man. "Don't tell me; tell God, Son, and don't be afraid to trust Him, for He will never fail you."

Back in the parlor with Sarah, Dad reached out and took her hand in his. "If I hadn't been true to God and myself last night—" He shuddered and, leaving the sentence unfinished, bowed his head reverently. It was all right now—all right!

Wedding by the Sea

ARTHUR GORDON

The wedding . . . it was not to be in a mighty cathedral with spires leaping heavenward; it was not to be in a warm brownstone church on the corner; it was not even to be in a tiny little chapel huddled in a quiet valley—rather, it was to be on a sandy beach with a barefoot bride and groom.

Would vows exchanged in such a setting mean as much as those spoken in a church of stone, steel, wood, and glass?

No one could possibly know—one could only hope.

Arthur Gordon (born 1912), during his long and memorable career, edited such renowned magazines as Good Housekeeping, Cosmopolitan, *and* Guideposts. *Somewhere along the way he found time to write full-length books and some of America's most cherished stories. Born on the Georgia seacoast, he never lost his love of those beaches he roamed as a child—as this story (popularized by* Reader's Digest *and Gordon's great story collection,* A Touch of Wonder*) so graphically reveals.*

FROM the start, they didn't want a formal wedding. No bridesmaids, no wedding march, nothing like that. "The old language and the old ritual are beautiful," our daughter said, "but they belong to millions of people. Ken and I want something of our own."

In an old town like ours, tradition binds with silver chains. "Well," we said a bit doubtfully, "it's your wedding. How do you want it, and when, and where?"

"At sundown," said Dana dreamily, shaking back her long blonde hair. "On the beach. As near the ocean as we can get. With a minister who understands how we feel and who can say some words that belong in the twentieth century."

"But what will you *wear?*" her mother asked, naturally.

"A long white dress," she said. "With a bouquet made of sea oats. But no shoes. I want to feel the sand under my feet. I don't know why—but I do."

She's choosing the beach, I said to myself, *because you taught her to love it. Some deep instinct in her knows that life makes tremendous silent statements where sand and saltwater meet. She's following that instinct, and she's right.*

So I was pleased, but still a faint strange sense of apprehension seemed to shadow the pleasure. Nothing to do with Ken—a fine boy, strong and tall, with a skilled surfer's easy grace, and a teaching career stretching out ahead of him. Nothing to do with anything graspable, really. *You're afraid*, I told myself finally—*that's it. Afraid that something very important in your life may be ending. Afraid that a closeness may be vanishing. You may be able to conceal the feeling, or even*

93

deny it, but you won't be able to push it away. It goes too deep for reason—or for words.

"Arrange for a big high tide, will you?" said Dana, giving us both a casual hug. "And no thunderstorms, please."

"I'm not entirely in charge of such things," I told her. "But we'll do the best we can."

The time came. We stood—friends, neighbors, relatives—in a little amphitheater made by the dunes. Behind us the dying sun hurled spears of amber light. Ahead, the ocean came surging joyously, all ivory and jade and gold. The young minister stood facing us, the crimson-lined hood of his robe fluttering in the wind, tongues of foam licking at his heels. He had to lift his voice above the clamor of the waves.

"Friends, we are here this afternoon to share with Ken and Dana a most important moment in their lives. In places like this they have learned to know and love each other. Now they have decided to live their lives together as husband and wife. . . ."

In places like this. . . . Under the overlay of time, I could feel the pictures form and dissolve in my mind. Years ago on this same beach, not many yards away, a placid pool left by the ebbing tide. One moment, a three-year-old playing at the edge. The next moment—incredibly—vanished. And the heart-stopping realization, the frantic plunge, the lunge that raised the small, dripping figure back into the sunlight, the overwhelming relief that somehow she had remembered what she had been taught about holding her

breath. Then the wide, gray eyes opening and the small, reproachful voice: "Why didn't you come *sooner?* It's all dark and bubbly down there!"

Or the day years later, when she was perhaps eleven or twelve, and we found the old pelican, sick and shivering. Nothing could be done; we had to watch him die. And the impact as death for the first time became a reality, and the piercing pain of compassion striking the unarmored spirit. "Oh," she said finally through her tears, groping for something to ease her anguish, "I'm glad we didn't know him very well."

And then, still later, the golden afternoons when she would go out saying gravely that she had to walk her dog, but knowing that we knew she really hoped to find Ken surfing. He was hardly aware of her then, but she would sit on a dune with arms clasped around her knees and her heart full of love and longing and the big German shepherd motionless as a statue by her side.

In places like this. . . . Why does time slide by so fast? I asked myself. Why does nothing stay?

Serenely the young minister's voice went on:

"We have been invited to hear Ken and Dana as they promise to face the future together, accepting whatever joy or sadness may lie ahead. These surroundings were not chosen by chance. Those who love the sea can hear in it the heartbeat of Creation as the tides ebb and flow, the sun rises and sets, and the stars come nightly to the sky. For the beauty around us, for the strength it offers, for the peace it brings, we are grateful."

Yes, I thought, *it is to find strength. To find endurance all we have to do is seek out places where great and elemental things prevail. For some of us the sea. For some the mountains, as the psalmist knew. I will lift up mine eyes. . . .*

Now the words were being spoken directly to the young couple:

"Dana and Ken, nothing is easier than saying words.

"Nothing is harder than living them, day after day.

"What you promise today must be renewed and redecided tomorrow and each day that stretches out before you.

"At the end of this ceremony, legally you will be man and wife, but still you must decide each day that you want to be married."

Can they understand that? I asked myself, watching the clear young profiles. *Can they possibly grasp it now? or will the realization take years, as it has for most of us, and then come so quietly that they're not even sure that it's there?*

The young minister was saying tenderly:

"All of us know that you are deeply in love. But beyond the warmth and glow, the excitement and romance, what is love, really?

"Real love is caring as much about the welfare and happiness of your marriage partner as about your own.

"Real love is not possessive or jealous; it is liberating; it sets you free to become your best self.

"Real love is not total absorption in each other; it is looking outward in the same direction—together.

"Love makes burdens lighter, because you divide them. It makes joys more intense, because you share them. It makes you stronger, so that you can reach out and become involved with life in ways you dared not risk alone."

True, I was thinking. *All true. But you can't learn it from hearing it. You have to learn it by living it, and even then no one but a saint can apply more than fragments of it to his own marriage or his own life. All we can do, even the best of us, is try. And even the trying is hard.*

Now the time had come for the questions, and indeed the language did belong to the twentieth century.

"Ken, will you take Dana to be your wife? Will you love and respect her? Will you be honest with her always? Will you stand by her through whatever may come? Will you make whatever adjustments are necessary so that you can genuinely share your life with her?"

"I will," said the tall boy, and to the same questions the slender girl gave the same answer.

Now the minister's steady gaze fell upon us.

"Who brings this woman to stand beside this man?"

"We do," my wife and I said together. We could not give our child away, for she was not our possession. She was uniquely and eternally herself. And yet, but for our own love, she would not be here under this tranquil sky, close to this restless sea.

The same question to Ken's parents. The same answer. And then a challenge to the four of us:

"Are you willing, now and always, to support and strengthen this marriage by upholding both Ken and Dana with your love and concern?"

"We are," we said, and now all of us were a part of the commitment. No favoritism. No side-taking.

Just a quiet, constant defense against the fierce centrifugal forces that threaten every marriage. *This at least*, I thought, *is wholly within our power; this much we can do.*

Now for a moment the wind seemed to hush itself, and around us the swaying sea oats grew almost still. I saw Dana's fingers tremble as she put her hand in Ken's, waiting for the ancient symbol of fidelity and love.

"I give you this ring," the tall boy said. "Wear it with love and joy. I choose you to be my wife this day and every day."

"I accept this ring," our child said in a small voice—but a woman's voice. "I will wear it with love and joy. I choose you to be my husband this day and every day."

Silence then, for a moment or two. No one stirred. The faces of the onlookers were touched with something indefinable, a kind of timelessness, a sense of life fulfilling itself and moving on. *Perhaps this is the way that everything of consequence begins*, I thought. *No certainty. No guarantees. Just a choice, an intention, a promise, a hope . . . .*

The minister reached forward and took the couple's clasped hands in his own.

"Ken and Dana, we have heard you promise to share your lives in marriage. We recognize and respect the covenant you have made. It's not a minister standing before you that makes your marriage real, but the honesty and sincerity of what you have said and done here before your friends and parents and in the sight of God. On behalf of all those present, I take your hands and acknowledge that you are husband and wife."

He smiled and released their hands.

"Now the ceremony is over, and the experience of living day by day as married people is about to begin. Go forth to meet it gladly. Love life, so that life will love you. The blessing of God be with you. So be it."

So be it, I thought, watching Dana kiss her husband and turn to embrace her mother. *So be it!* cried all the hugs and the handshakes, the excited laughter and the unashamed tears. *So be it*, murmured the wind and the waves, turning away once more from human things.

And when I looked for the apprehension that had been in me, it was gone.

To the Victor

ALICE GORTON WYNN

All too often in life, success comes because of who we know rather than what we know. It comes because of "pull" rather than performance. Thus the already crowned victor is likely to continue raking in a disproportionate percentage of the spoils.

Equally unfortunate, far too few of us equate success with character, with inner self-worth. To young Dr. Ben Bradley, judging by appearances, his father's life and career were evidently a failure. And now his father's lack of success was going to spill over on him as well. It was sad, but it was the way things were done. It was life—but it wasn't fair!

IT was supper time and the second day after he had returned from Lee Medical School. Dr. Ben Bradley smiled indulgently as he turned into Hale Street and came to his father's odds-and-ends clothing store.

Although it was past closing time, Ben knew that he would find his father waiting on a late customer or doddering over his unfathomable ledger. The yellow paint on the shop had worn through to the more ancient brown. Cheap, ready-made clothes hung for-lornly in the dim window. Inside, one needed a guide to steer a course through heaps of everything for men, piled on rickety tables and packing boxes.

The elderly Bradley was seated at his desk, his head bowed over his books. As Ben saw him, an old grammar-school poem flashed into his mind, and he thought, *If the recording angel is still listing names in the "book of gold," that venerable chap, Ben Adhem, has nothing on my dad.*

William Bradley closed his ledger and looked up, a worn, commonplace little man in a threadbare coat.

"Six o'clock," Ben reminded.

"Yes, I know. I'm all ready to leave, Son."

"Been looking at offices on Commercial Avenue," Ben said. "Rent's pretty steep, but I guess the old burg's grown a lot in a year."

"Perhaps you'd do better to locate in a new place." Bradley's voice sounded tired.

Ben stopped rearranging the pile of underwear on the counter. "Why, Dad! You always said you wanted me to practice right here."

"Of course I'd rather have you home, Ben. It's been lonesome since your mother died. But I've made such a botch of my life here in Evansport that the name of Bradley's a laughingstock. You'd only be handicapped by it if you opened up here."

Ben whisked up a man's suit that had been flung across a chair and slipped it upon its hanger. "Oh, those queer ideas of yours, Dad!" he scolded. "You've done lots of good, but you haven't made enough noise about it. That's what gets most folks by."

After they had seen to the army of rusty locks and bolts, Ben took his father's arm, and they started for home.

"The question is, Ben, will people trust their sick to the son of a ne'er-do-well? Public sentiment is strong. Folks will link you with me ready enough and put you down as a chip off the old irrational Bradley stump!"

"Mighty fine stock, I'll say."

"It hurts me most because I've never been able to do much for you, Son. I've lain awake nights, too. That time you needed help most, when those notes I endorsed came due. Remember?"

Ben squared his shoulders. "Someday I'll get even with those good-for-nothing rascals that plucked you," he declared.

"I guess they'd have paid if they could, Ben. One had an invalid wife, and the other was burned out of house and home." As they were turning into Commercial Avenue, gay music filled their ears, and decorations on buildings as far as they could see down the avenue brought a startled look to William Bradley's eyes. "This is the day!" he cried. "James Mallory's coming back. I almost forgot."

"Do you remember him, Dad?"

"Remember him? Yes—yes, indeed." He chuckled to himself. "It's been a long time, though. He's a millionaire now. Guess he's forgotten me."

Like a guardian castle on an outlying hill stood the home for friendless boys which Mallory had recently built and endowed. This evening the great financier would present it to the town. There would be a rousing big meeting in the auditorium of the institution, with speeches and music. The welcoming committee was on its way now to the station to meet Mallory. Ben and his father stopped, arm in arm, to watch the procession.

Right behind the band of music rode Clinton Rand, owner of a chain of restaurants. His car stopped before the Pilgard Building. On a street-floor window was conspicuous lettering freshly done. "Clinton Rand Jr., M.D." Young Rand hurried out and climbed into a seat beside his father.

Ben Bradley laughed. "They're going to meet Mallory and drive him to the banquet hall! Then sit with him on the platform!"

"His money does it, Ben. Money always does."

"And young Clint's after the appointment of resident doctor at Mallory's new institution, I'm sure," Ben observed. "There'll be a fine office for him, operating rooms, and a good salary."

"Oh, Ben, if you could get that place," Bradley sighed.

"Might as well cry for the moon."

"But you sent in your application with a statement about your standing and experience?" Bradley asked anxiously.

"Yes, but there are a dozen applicants. I stand just as much chance of seeing a million-dollar bill. Clint Rand will win out. His father's sure to be on the board of management."

"But Clint couldn't touch your work," Bradley persisted.

"He skimmed through."

"And I can remember when Clint's father ran one little restaurant on Mill Street," Bradley said resignedly.

"Everybody's forgotten that. Success is a powerful narcotic. Now Rand's the richest man in town, with a mansion on the Highlands and the biggest hotel named for him."

William Bradley cleared his throat with an effort. "It does look as if common old drudgery doesn't count for much these days."

"Well, never mind," Ben encouraged. "I wouldn't swap you for—for—anyway, come on, or we'll be late for supper. I'm hungry."

In half an hour they were at home. It was an old place, one of the oldest, its pillars decaying and its walls streaked by rain and dust. As they opened the front door, the odor of cooking food floated heavily from the kitchen.

Aunt Nannie, who had kept house since Ben's mother died, came from the kitchen. "You're late again, of course," she fretted. "Supper's spoiled, trying to keep it warm."

"Don't cross her," Bradley admonished Ben with a chuckle. "But she's not well, poor soul."

Ben looked over the mail and found a letter for his father.

"Open it, Ben," Bradley said without looking up.

"It's an invitation, Dad, to the grand doings tonight."

"Well, I declare!" William Bradley adjusted his spectacles and read through the typewritten page. He pointed to the signature. "Whose name is that? I wonder. Never heard of it."

"Of course, it's just a form invitation sent out by the town boosters," Ben explained. "Naturally they want a crowd to greet this great man. We'd better go. Don't see celebrities like Mallory every day."

Ben ran up to his room. At the door he paused and looked around. A ragged hole gaped in the matting beside the bed. The paper was mildewed and bulging in places. The bureau had a crack running diagonally across the mirror. Ben remembered that his father had bought it to oblige a neighbor who was moving to a distant town and wished to sell his household furniture.

Poor Dad! he thought. *Any person who has a hard-luck story gets by with him. Any ragtag can get credit at his store. Bless his foolish, old-fashioned heart! I ought to scold him for his own good, but it would break his heart.*

Ben seized the brush and gave his brown hair quick, backward strokes. *Leave him and go to a new place? I guess not! He needs me. I'll launch out right here, and we'll sink or swim together.*

William Bradley ate little at supper. Soon he laid down his knife and fork and leaned back in his chair. There was wistfulness in his eyes as he spoke.

"You don't know how glad I was when you picked out medicine, Ben. I never mentioned it, but I always wanted to be a doctor myself. It seemed like the best way to help folks." He laughed, embarrassed. "I hankered after it so, it took me a long time to give up the idea. Maybe that's why I made such a fizzle of things. But circumstances in our family kept me from fulfilling my ambition. I had to look out for the others. For years I taught night school extra to help out with the expenses."

Ben glanced at his watch. "Seven-thirty. We'd better start."

They joined the tide that swept toward the great structure on the hill and visited the gardens, swimming pool, gymnasium, and workshop. They were conducted through the homelike bedrooms, the library, and the hospital.

Ben's father glowed with approval as he sat down in one of the library chairs and looked about at the revolving shelves, the low tables, and the soft lights.

"Mallory's done great things," he said. "It's wonderful."

But Ben feasted his eyes in the hospital. He pictured suffering faces against white pillows, invalids in rolling chairs, and efficient nurses bringing health and happiness to their charges.

"What a place to work in!" he cried. "Everything one needs. What a chance for young Rand!"

Now they were seated in the rear of the auditorium, just as Mallory arrived. Beaming with importance, Clinton Rand ushered him in and to the stage. He was introduced and made ready to speak.

"Whew! I'd hate to get him down on *me*," Ben whispered. "Look at those gray eyes, Dad."

His father did not answer. He was listening intently as Mallory began. First he spoke of boys in general, their chances and their futures. He described the endless struggle of some and the need of a helping hand. Then his voice changed, and his eyes narrowed.

"This evening," he continued, "I propose to travel back about twenty years and tell of an incident that was staged right here in Evansport. It will include some personal history, but I offer no apology."

William Bradley settled back comfortably, a hand to his ear.

"My parents were Irish emigrants," Mallory said. "They died of fever within a few days of each other and left me an orphan at fourteen. Undersized and underfed, I couldn't do the hard work in the fields; so I wandered into town. Walking the streets of Evansport, I was discouraged and almost done for. Finally I somehow got a place as chore boy in a restaurant."

Mallory's voice lowered, but it could be heard to the farthest corner of the hall.

"Whenever the preacher talks about perdition, there comes to me a vision of that restaurant kitchen. Twelve hours a day I slaved there. The others relieved their ill tempers by cursing and cuffing me.

"One night I stumbled and dropped a tureen of boiling soup. The proprietor rushed in to see what the trouble was. I tried to apologize, but he cursed and booted me out of the door."

Ben Bradley felt as if he were on the highest end of a seesaw and might come down any minute, so eager was he to hear the climax of Mallory's story. He glanced at his father and saw burning eyes in a white face.

Mallory's voice softened. The hard lines about the mouth relaxed to a smile. "I must have been an awful sight sitting there on the curb—unkempt, discouraged, a mere child. Just then somebody put a hand on my head and asked me what was the matter. I looked up into wonderful gray-blue eyes belonging to a young man. He had some books under his arm. But his face! It brought warm hope and encouragement to me. I tried to tell him my troubles; but I was only a youngster, so I did just what a little boy would do; I burst out crying.

"This young man made believe to scold me a little, then told me to never mind. He took me home with him and fixed me up in every way. I remember that his house wasn't much for elegance, but it looked like heaven to me. I had a bath and a clean bed, something to eat, and plenty of helpful, inspiring words."

Mallory sighed as if with the bittersweet memories of the old struggling days.

"I'm not sure that my protector saw any promise in the forlorn creature he had befriended, but he didn't go halfway. Taking me to his shop next day, he fitted me out with decent clothes. Then he got me a job in a machine shop. I studied in his night school free of charge."

Ben felt his father's trembling hand resting over his own.

"Twelve years later," Mallory finished, "I sent him a check for one thousand dollars, but the Post Office returned the letter unclaimed. Recently I learned that my benefactor had returned to Evansport. I have traveled two thousand miles to see him. I had my secretary send him a special invitation to this meeting. This man I've been talking about is William Bradley, and I want him to come right up here to the platform. William Bradley, with his wonderful, great heart, put me just where I am today."

When Ben's father arose, trembling, wondering, happy, and started forward, Evansport waited a full half minute to grasp it all.

Then Evansport arose, too, and opened its heart and lungs to William Bradley. All except Clinton Rand, the restaurant owner, who had hired the orphan boy twenty years ago.

And Ben Bradley's throat ached with the pain of happiness. There stood his own father up there beside the millionaire Mallory! And his father had been a failure, so folks said.

What was Mallory saying now? Ben struggled nearer to the stage.

"The name of this institution shall be The Bradley Home for Boys."

Ben's father lifted his head proudly. The weary look was gone from his face. But Mallory was speaking again, gripping William Bradley's hand.

"I hope your business is in shape to leave because I have set my heart on other work for you. I've had a cottage built on these grounds for your private use. Take personal charge of the library. Keep open house there. Choose the books and periodicals that will make my boys good citizens.

"And now about your son. I've noticed his application among the others for the position of resident physician to the institution. Because of my priceless obligations to you and knowing that the boy must have inherited the father's great qualities, I have appointed him to the position in question."

As they walked homeward under the protecting trees along Evergreen Street, father and son were silent. Then they stopped suddenly, as if with the same idea. Ben placed his hands upon his father's shoulders and drew him closer.

"Oh, Dad, to think—to think—that it's you, *my* father! You're the greatest man in the world."

"Hush, boy," the father reprimanded him tenderly. "Nonsense! Things just came out right; that's all. Now I can hold up my old head before folks. In my son's sight I'm a success. That's what counts most."

The Tiger

MARY DIRLAM

*Few individuals make more of a difference in our life—
for good or ill—than our teachers. After the age of six,
we are with them as much, if not more, than we are
with our parents.*

*Teachers, like all mortals, yearn to be appreciated,
liked, loved, yet it is the nature of the business they are
in that they often have to choose between popularity and
its opposite, knowing deep down that an ounce of
long-term respect and appreciation is worth a ton of
short-term popularity.*

*Occasionally during the swift-flying years, our lives
are enriched by mentors with tough love, teachers
willing to be misunderstood so that the student is not
wrecked on the shoals of premature adulation or
egocentricity.*

Mark Spencer found that out too late.

IT seemed to Mark Spencer that in this room, at
this moment, he had reached a pausing point. One
phase of his life was over; another was about to begin.

His artist's eye took in the element of design in his
immediate surroundings. There, sitting across the
desk from him, was Dean Harber—all angles this
man, with his wiry, energetic body. Through the
window were the familiar outlines of the Bryant Art
School buildings, which had been Mark's home for
the past four years. On Harber's desk was the large
rectangular folder marked "Spencer."

Harber leafed idly through the folder before he
spoke. Then he looked up to smile at the young man
who sat opposite him. "Well, here we are, Mark," he
said. "You're through with us now—it's time. You've
learned what we could teach you here. The rest will
be work, experience—development."

"I know," Mark murmured. He watched in a detached way as the dean continued to leaf through his
paintings. These papers and canvases were his
achievements, the products of all the years during
which he had known he was going to become an
artist.

Dean Harber pulled out a watercolor from the
folder and nodded in response. "Yes," he said. "You'll
make the grade. They'll recognize you slowly—the
artists first, then the critics. Sooner or later the public will catch on, too."

"Why are you looking at that landscape?" Mark questioned. "It's one of my high school things. A bad job."

"It has faults," Harber replied. "Labored—muddy.
Yet there's something in it, too. Your high school
work has always interested me, you know. It has ever
since that day when your first folder came into my
office." He put the watercolor down and fell into a
reminiscent mood. "That folder—'Mark Spencer,

Fairview High School, age 17.' We had hundreds of high school folders that year. But yours had something different about it. Yours showed development, the ability to learn—to go from good to better. Do you know what else it showed?"

"No," said Mark. "What else?"

"A teacher. I've always wanted to ask you about that teacher. Whoever he was, he knew what you could do and how to get it out of you."

"Old Greenbaum," Mark said softly, "Thomas J. Greenbaum. But—"

"But what?" asked Harber.

"I don't know what I was going to say exactly." Mark laughed. "Except that Greenbaum, my high school art teacher, wasn't the kind of man you seem to think he was. He was a tiger. I really hated him. He always had it in for me, you see. He was fairly decent with most of the others, but everything I did was wrong. Whenever I tried to meet him halfway, he'd always lash back at me with some sarcastic remark—putting me in my place. It always seemed as though he tried to be as unpleasant as he could."

Mark paused, staring at the watercolor which Harber had taken out of his folder. It was indeed a bad job—clumsy, uncertain; but he hadn't thought so at the time. It had taken Mark years to learn how to criticize his own work. Back in high school, every painting he'd done had seemed special and wonderful to him—even this watercolor.

Mark remembered the day in June, four years ago, when he had put this same watercolor into the folder that was going to Bryant Art School. It had been just the day before commencement, and classes at Fairview had already ended for the school year. Mark, all his thoughts bent on his urgent desire to win the Bryant four-year scholarship, had come into the school art studio to assemble the last of the paintings and drawings that he would submit to Bryant as examples of his work. He had been holding the watercolor admiringly before him, pleased as he always was with what he had done, when Old Greenbaum entered the room.

"I am sorry," Greenbaum commented acidly, "to interrupt this touching scene between the artist and his work. I hope I don't intrude."

Mark flushed, putting the watercolor down on the table. Old Tiger Greenbaum and his poisonous tongue. Well, he wasn't going to have to put up with it much longer.

Greenbaum walked over to the painting and looked at it critically. "All blobbed up," he said dryly. "I wonder if you'll ever get over thinking that watercolor is oil paint."

"Listen, Mr. Greenbaum," Mark began, "I—"

Greenbaum interrupted as though Mark had not spoken. His gnarled index finger traced a line over the painting. "From there to there," he said in his rasping, metallic voice, "it's messy, undecided. Over here," he observed, pointing to another section, "the color looks as if it had been scrubbed with a wash brush." He seemed to hesitate for a moment. "The tree," he added grudgingly, "the tree is good."

Mark tried to swallow down his anger, as he had so many times before in the course of that year. He had bit his lips and said nothing on all those occasions when Greenbaum had made him do sketch after sketch of the same subject—refusing to admit, even when Mark was certain that what he had done was flawless, that it could not be done better. He had worked in silent rage on difficult projects in perspective which he had no desire to attempt but which Greenbaum had insisted that he do. He had, more times than he could remember, resisted the temptation to throw his brush or charcoal stick in Greenbaum's face.

It had been necessary, Mark thought, that he should control his ever-mounting resentment of this inflexible, unsympathetic teacher. He couldn't afford to "tell him off" and to drop his course in art. For Mark knew, and had never questioned, that he must become a painter. That meant he must go to art school, and to go to art school, his high school record must be as superior as he could make it. There would be no art school for him without a scholarship—and no scholarship without real accomplishment in his high school art courses.

But now the school year was over. Whatever Old Greenbaum had had to say about Mark had already been said on the little blank which Bryant Art School sent to the teachers of scholarship candidates. And Mark was bitterly certain that Greenbaum's recommendation had been, at best, a halfhearted one.

He grabbed his watercolor from the table, where Greenbaum was standing before it. "I'm afraid I'm not interested in the rest of your criticism, Mr. Greenbaum," he said heatedly. "We're parting company now, and I can't say I'm sorry. You've never liked me—I don't know why, and I don't care any more. It goes without saying that I haven't liked you much, either. If I hadn't known, if I hadn't been sure, that I'm good, you would have discouraged me from ever going on with art. Maybe that's what you were trying to do, but I—"

Greenbaum, his face impassive, broke in on the angry boy before him. "But you never questioned your talent. We both know that. You've always been

certain of yourself, of your paintings. In your own opinion, you could do no wrong."

"Come off it!" Mark retorted, forgetting in his emotion that he was talking to a teacher. "You must have known, even if you wouldn't admit it, that I'm as good a student as you've had at Fairview. You were standing right here in this room when Gustav Scholl told us both that I was one of the most promising students he'd seen in this country."

Gustav Scholl was a distinguished German painter who had visited Fairview High School earlier in the year at Greenbaum's invitation. At the time, Greenbaum had unbent enough to make a special point of showing Mark's work to Scholl, and Scholl's reaction had been one of glowing enthusiasm. "My friend," he'd said, grabbing Greenbaum's arm in excitement, "this young man will do fine things!"

Now Mr. Greenbaum's lips pulled into a tight line as he said, "Ah, yes, our exuberant friend Scholl! His mistimed admiration did you a wrong, I think. He gave you that much more reason to believe in your own superiority."

Mark stuffed the last of his paintings into his folder. "And that," he replied, "is more than you've ever done for me. A complete stranger walking into this studio for a few minutes—and he gave me more encouragement than you've given me in a whole year. I could add," he said bitingly, "that Scholl's name means a good bit more in the world of art than your own."

A shadow of pain passed over Greenbaum's face before he smiled the odd, stiff smile that Mark had come to know and mistrust. But he made no answer, and Mark took advantage of the pause to pick up his folder and leave the room.

Once out in the bright June sunshine, walking for the last time down the path that led from the art studio to the main building of Fairview High School, Mark experienced a twinge of regret. Maybe he shouldn't have been so rough on Greenbaum. There was no longer any point in nursing the grievances that had built up during the past year. Still, he couldn't believe that he had been unfair. Perhaps he'd even done some good. Greenbaum might think over what Mark had said to him and might recognize the justice of it.

Actually, Mark admitted to himself, Greenbaum was all right with the usual run of students. Most of the boys and girls at Fairview liked him. He was patient and gentle with the pupil who could hardly handle a brush, always encouraging to the awkward student who showed scattered signs of improvement. Why had he chosen Mark as his particular victim? Mark could only believe that it was jealousy—jealousy at discovering a teenager who already had more ability than Greenbaum himself possessed at the age of fifty-eight. . . .

It had all been so long ago—not long as years go, but long in experience. Now, sitting in Dean Harber's office, Mark found it hard to remember all the details of that year before he had been awarded the scholarship to Bryant Art School. At Bryant he had worked hard, won three major prizes, even sold one or two of his oil paintings. When his class graduated next week, he would be announced as the winner of a two-year traveling fellowship to France. There he would study with Gustav Scholl himself, who now had a studio in Paris. Fairview High and Greenbaum seemed far away.

"You've changed, you know," Harber said suddenly. "My only doubt about giving you that scholarship in 1948 was a personal one. When you came to interview me, you were cocky—too sure of yourself. Now you're still sure of yourself, as you ought to be. But you've learned to take criticism and to know what your limitations are."

Mark grinned. "Come to think of it," he said, "I suppose I was pretty unbearable during that interview. This teacher I just mentioned to you—Greenbaum—may have been partly responsible. I got so little praise from him that I felt I had to blow my own horn."

"Greenbaum?" asked Dean Harber, raising his eyebrows. "Greenbaum never praised you?"

"Why, no," Mark answered. "As I say, he always had it in for me."

Harber rose from his desk and walked over to a filing cabinet. After leafing through several folders, he finally pulled out a piece of paper. "Read this," he suggested, handing it to Mark.

Mark took the paper, unfolded it carefully, and read.

Fairview High School
Fairview, Ohio
Department of Art

June 30, 1948

Dear Dean Harber:

I presume upon your time to write this letter about Mark Spencer, a candidate for the Bryant Art School four-year scholarship, because I feel that the answers to questions on the standard blank do not fully suggest this boy's unusual qualifications.

You have already had one interview with Mark Spencer. I daresay that you found him vain of his talents, overconfident of his prospects. I have found him so, too, and have done what I could to discourage these traits.

I hope I am not out of order if I suggest that this impression is a misleading one. Mark Spencer's faults, such as they are, are the faults of a boy whose talent is truly extraordinary. He is still young; he will grow up; and I am confident that he will become a distinguished artist. If he is too ready to acknowledge his own ability, it is only because that ability is great and is so much the center of his life and ambitions. He is compelled, more than the ordinary person, to believe in himself.

Throughout his high school years, Mark Spencer has never been sure that he would be able to continue his study of art. There is little money in his family, and his chance to succeed at what he wants most to do depends entirely upon the recognition he can win from such "powers" as you represent. Once he is assured that his chance will be given him, he will be less insecure, more able to take criticism and to be what he has it in him to be.

I do not urge that your scholarship be awarded to Mark Spencer for personal reasons; his talent is too pronounced to make that necessary. But I do urge that his candidacy should not, for personal reasons, be viewed with disfavor.

> *Very truly yours,*
> *Thomas J. Greenbaum*

"It was this letter," Dean Harber observed as Mark finished reading, "that helped to clear away my last doubts as to the advisability of awarding you the Bryant scholarship. I was convinced that your Mr. Greenbaum knew the boy he spoke of. And," Harber added, smiling, "I wasn't wrong."

Mark, staring at the letter, didn't reply. June 30, 1948—the date on the letterhead—that would have been four, possibly five, days after the June afternoon on which he had given Old Greenbaum a piece of his mind. Then Greenbaum had written this letter. Unhappily, Mark wondered whether he himself could ever write such a letter after such an incident.

His eye caught one of Greenbaum's phrases and fixed on it—"to be what he has it in him to be." That was how it was, then. More than Scholl, more than even Mark himself, Old Greenbaum must have had a high vision of what Mark had it in him to be, a vision so determined that he was willing to sacrifice his student's affection for himself as a teacher in order to further his future as an artist.

"You say that Greenbaum 'had it in' for you," Harber observed. "I can see from your expression that this

letter has suggested otherwise. Why don't you let me give you an extra ticket for the commencement exercises?" he suggested. "I have an idea that Mr. Thomas Greenbaum would be the proudest man in the auditorium if he could see you walk across that platform as the winner of the two-year fellowship to Paris."

Mark looked up, his face red, as he put the letter back on Harber's desk. Harber was right—he knew that now. No one he had known in his life would be so proud of his present success as Old Greenbaum. No one he had known deserved so well to be proud.

Mark's glance fell again on the old watercolor which Harber had pulled out of his folder. He would never again, he reflected, look at this watercolor without a stab of regret. The quality of design which he had sensed at the beginning of this interview had taken on a dreadful symmetry.

Vividly remembered images from the past flooded before him. Greenbaum's knobby finger on his work: "Erase those lines—do it again—you can do in one line what you've done in several." Greenbaum's cool, appraising eyes taking in a finished sketch: "Not bad—and not so good as you think it is, either." And then the image which came not from memory but from imagination: an old man sitting down to write a letter full of understanding and faith.

"Shall we send him a ticket?" the dean was saying.

Mark shook his head. For no ticket could now be sent—no grateful gesture was any longer possible.

"Thank you, Dean Harber," he said. "I wish I could. But Mr. Greenbaum died two years ago."

Kathleen's Gold Piece

CHRISTINE WHITING PARAMETER

Poor Kathleen! She had to leave college because dear Father had been gulled again. After two other disasters, he had co-signed again—with the same results. And now it looked like they'd lose everything: Dad's business, all his assets, even the home they lived in. How could he?

Yet on the train, Kathleen realized by her own actions that she was her father's daughter: Trust she must, though she, too, lost heavily.

But the last chapter had not yet been written.

Christine Whiting Parameter (1877–1953) early in this century was one of America's most beloved writers of inspirational literature. Today most of that fame is gone, and she is remembered for but one story, "David's Star of Bethlehem," one of the greatest Christmas stories ever written. This almost forgotten story reveals what we have been missing and why her voice should still be heard.

As the train passed through the familiar town, Kathleen Monroe leaned forward in her seat, catching her breath sharply to keep back the tears. She watched the library flash by, with the old town clock capping its stone tower; the station, its platform piled high with trunks because spring vacation began tomorrow; and at last the tall, stately buildings of the college itself, standing serenely beautiful amid their setting of green woodland and greener lawns.

They were past now, and Kathleen sank back against the cushions and closed her eyes. She would never see them again, she thought drearily. She had left a day before the other girls, because she couldn't bear the thought of their gay farewells with promises of speedy meetings. Besides, she wanted these hours on the train free from companionship. She wanted to get her bearings, to be able to greet her family with a smile. They must not know, most of all her father must not guess, how hard it was for her to give up college.

She drew her mother's letter from her pocket and read the words again, although she knew them almost by heart. It was the old story of her lovable, kindhearted father signing a note. This was the third time in Kathleen's memory that he had come to grief by such an action, only this time the result was more serious. It meant leaving the home which had been laboriously paid for and seeking smaller quarters. It meant also the loss of certain advantages for the small brother and sister—and no college for Kathleen. Ted, her older brother, could work his way through college, but Kathleen would be needed at home. Her mother was far from strong, and a maid would be out of the question until her father had gained another start.

Kathleen's heart contracted at the thought. Another start would not be easy for a man past fifty. Her mother wrote that he had promised solemnly never to sign another note. Well, thought the girl grimly, it would be easy for a man who had lost almost everything to keep that promise! A man with a family had no right to do such things!

For a moment a little flare of anger possessed her, which melted suddenly as her father's face rose before her. She remembered those kindly, trusting eyes, which saw only the best in everyone, and knew instantly that she wouldn't have her father different, though, as Ted once remarked, "Dad was too easy." The family were always using poor grades of shoe polish or matches because some hard-luck story had pierced his heart. No tramp left the door unfed if Dad happened to be at home. He had been known to give his good overcoat to a poor wretch he found shivering on a corner selling shoestrings. He had bought the shoestrings, too, thought the girl, with a choking laugh of reminiscence. They were impossible shoestrings. Ted had donated them to a rummage sale!

Suddenly Kathleen's heart lightened. She did not know that she had inherited her father's optimistic nature. There were worse things than giving up college and doing housework! She believed she was hungry. Her roommate, Sally King, had insisted on giving her a box lunch. She had put it up herself in the Agora Kitchen. Sally was the only girl who knew that Kathleen would not return after vacation and had assured her jestingly that she had salted her sandwiches with her tears.

It was a generous lunch, dainty and attractive, enough for two meals at least, which was thoughtful of Sally, thought Kathleen gratefully. She looked about and saw that the Pullman was almost empty. Everyone had flown to the diner at first call for supper, save a little old lady across the way. As Kathleen lifted one of Sally's delicious sandwiches from the box, she glanced across the aisle to find the old lady regarding her in real distress, and laying her lunch box down, she crossed the aisle.

"Is there anything I can do for you?" she asked courteously.

"I don't know what to do," answered the lady nervously. "I'm not used to traveling alone. My son Tom expected to come as far as Buffalo, but at the last minute things came up to change his plans. He went to New York yesterday. Then Phoebe—she's Tom's wife—expected to see me aboard the train, but she was taken ill, and the girls were both off for over Sunday, so she sent for a taxi and arranged for the driver to make me comfortable. He was very attentive, followed me right aboard and everything, but just now, when I looked in my bag, I found my pocketbook was gone."

"Too bad!" exclaimed Kathleen in great sympathy. "Have you looked everywhere?"

"Everywhere. My ticket was in the bag, but I

haven't a penny—not a penny!" she repeated soberly. "I'm going to Evanston, but—"

Her voice trembled, and Kathleen said quickly, "Don't worry. The first thing to do is to have supper. Lucky enough, I have enough for two. I will bring it over here, and we'll have a cozy time together. Then I'll look for your purse. Mother says I am splendid about finding things."

The old lady brightened visibly, and Kathleen saw with pleasure that she thoroughly enjoyed the sandwiches, although she protested at first about accepting them. Meanwhile, the girl was making calculations. She had only enough money to see her through, but of course, she must look out for the old lady who was, Kathleen noticed, dressed very simply. The loss of her money might mean very much to her. The taxi driver might have stolen it, or she might have dropped it in the cab. It was plain she was easily upset. Now if the purse remained lost—

Well, it did. Their supper over, Kathleen moved the old lady across the aisle and made a thorough search, and the porter helped; but all in vain, and the old lady's distress grew more apparent. It was then that Kathleen remembered her "lucky piece." It was a ten-dollar gold piece her father had given her on her eighteenth birthday, and she had never spent it. She had kept it carefully in her purse, carefully wrapped in a paper, much against the advice of her small but cautious brother who declared she would lose it before she had a chance to spend it. Kathleen replied she was keeping it for luck, and as the months

passed, she went without things rather than use it. It must be confessed that she felt a tinge of regret at the thought of parting with it, but there was no other way. She produced the gold piece, which her elderly friend thankfully accepted along with Kathleen's card.

"I'll mail a check as soon as I get home, dear," she promised gratefully. "You're sure you can spare it?"

"Quite sure. I wasn't counting on it at all," answered Kathleen honestly. "Do you want to rest now, or shall we talk awhile?"

The old lady smiled brightly. "I'd love to talk; but you mustn't feel obliged to bother with an old woman, though goodness knows what I would have done without you! I told Tom next time he wanted to see his mother he'd have to come to her. I'm too old to travel. I guess I've proved it—and once I get home I'm going to stay there. After all, there *is* no place like home."

The words brought a warm thrill to Kathleen's heart. "I'm going home, too," she said gently. "I can hardly wait to see them all, and I think I will stay there for some time to come."

The old lady had bright, shrewd eyes, which somehow reminded the girl of an English sparrow. She turned them on Kathleen now as she replied, "I sort of thought you were from college and going home for vacation."

Kathleen smiled. "I am, but—"

Afterward Kathleen couldn't have told how it happened. As a rule she was rather reticent about her own affairs, but there seemed to be something very appealing in the old lady's face, and before bedtime she knew all Kathleen's troubles: how Dad had signed the note just because he was the most trusting, easily imposed on, dearest father in the world; how Ted must work his way through college; how the home must be given up; and how Dad's business would have to go unless a miracle occurred to clear the skies. Kathleen did not realize that she was making light of her own part of the trouble, but as she finished speaking, the old lady said gently, "So you're not going back to college?"

"No," answered the girl gravely. "I'll be needed at home. Mother can't manage everything alone, and perhaps I'll find time for some outside work. I want to earn something so the younger ones won't have to go without things. I haven't had time for any plans, but I'm sure there's a way, if only I can find it; and I wouldn't for worlds have Father know how much I really care for college. I'm hoping he'll somehow save the business. It does seem as if a man as good and honest as Father ought not to fail just because he does a kindness to someone. Well, you must get off to bed, and so must I. I—I—hope I haven't bored you. Somehow it's made me happier to talk."

"Indeed, you haven't bored me!" responded the old lady quickly. "You've made me feel like a real grandma. Tom's girls were all so busy they didn't have much time for me. Not that I blame them, child. It's natural for young folks to flock together. Good night, my dear. Sweet dreams!"

She looked up so wistfully that the girl stopped impulsively for a good-night kiss.

Kathleen was right. Her talk *had* eased her heart, and she slept well. The train was leaving Buffalo as she awoke. Her first thought was of her old friend, and that she must be ready to escort her to the dining car for breakfast. When she was dressed, however, she was surprised to find the section opposite ready for the day—and vacant.

"Is my lady in the dining car?" she asked the porter.

"You mean that old lady what lost the pocketbook?" he asked. "She done leave the train at Buffalo, Miss."

"What!" gasped Kathleen. "She was on her way to Evanston!"

"No, ma'am. She done got off in Buffalo. She gave me half a dollar when she left, so she must ha' found her purse all right. I'll fix your section, Miss, while you's in the diner."

"I—I guess I won't go to the diner," said Kathleen weakly. "I have some sandwiches, and—"

She didn't finish the sentence. She sat down where she had sat with the old lady and stared at the landscape with unseeing eyes. Could it be possible that the sweet old lady was an imposter? Yet she had said distinctly that she was going to Evanston, and she wouldn't have needed the ten dollars had Buffalo been her destination. Suddenly Kathleen smiled. If she had been taken in, she was only following in her father's footsteps. How quickly Dad would have come to the rescue of the old dear! Then at the thought of the old lady's face her own brightened up. Of course she was all right! It was all very strange, but Kathleen believed in her. It was fortunate that it was her own lucky piece she had parted with. She needn't tell the family about it.

But Kathleen was counting without the family. She received a joyous welcome, all the more joyous because of the dark days that preceded it. She wondered, as she looked around on the adoring faces lifted to her that night at supper, how she could have thought anything about a hardship when she belonged to such a family. She was questioned about every minute of her trip, and before she knew it she had told about the old lady and the lucky piece. "Perhaps I was foolish," she explained hurriedly, "but she was all alone. It would have been dreadful not to help her."

"I said you'd lose that gold piece," proclaimed small David.

"She hasn't lost it, Sonny," said her father quietly. "She's passed it on. I'm glad you did, Kathleen. I'd have been ashamed of you if you hadn't. The prospects don't look very bright, but if you never hear from that old lady, I'll see that you get another lucky piece, though you may have to wait some time for it. You wouldn't have been my daughter if you hadn't helped the poor soul, would she, Mother?"

"Not *your* daughter, surely," said Mother, smiling.

Yet as the days passed and no word came from the old lady, Kathleen began to blame herself for her sudden generosity. Her father had suddenly aged by this last blow. He was working early and late in an attempt to save the business, and when the girl saw how many things her mother had done without, she realized that even ten dollars would have helped.

She had been at home two weeks when one evening her father burst in upon them as they sat down to supper. They all realized at once that something unusual had occurred, because, though he was evidently trying to be calm, Dad was the sort who couldn't possibly keep any good news to himself. It took great self-control for him to hand Kathleen a letter and ask her to read it to the family. She took it wonderingly, but when she saw the cramped writing, she exclaimed, "It's from my old lady! And—where did you get it, Dad? And—"

"Oh, read it, read it!" commanded Father. "Then I'll explain—"

He stopped, because Kathleen had obeyed him, and even the children leaned forward on their elbows in expectation.

My Dear Little Friend:

I wonder what you are thinking of me for taking French leave of you! You may be calling me all sorts of disgraceful names, but I'm hoping that, although appearances are certainly against me, you've kept just a grain of faith in the old woman you befriended so generously. I saw you unwrap that gold piece from its tissue paper, child, and I knew it was something precious—a lucky piece, most likely; and after you left me for the night, I got to wondering if I couldn't make it a real lucky piece—one you'd never forget.

For you see, your story sounded very natural. There was a time when I went through just such ups and downs, because my husband, like your father, would always believe the best of folks, even when there wasn't

much "best" to believe. So I saw it all very clearly. I knew just what you were going through, you and your mother, and your father, too. I don't know but what his part was the hardest.

First I thought that, if I could afford it, I'd send you back to college, and then I knew that wouldn't help because you said they needed you at home. Then I thought of lots of other things which did not suit me; and then, just as I was getting disgusted with myself as a fairy godmother, I had a wonderful idea. You see, my son Tom is in the same line of business your father is. He's been branching out lately, and only a few days before, I had heard him say he wished he knew of the right man for his western office, one he could trust absolutely. Well, I knew from what you said that your father was one to be trusted; and I knew also that Tom would be in Buffalo that night. Do you see now what I was up to?

Of course, my dear, a letter to Tom wouldn't have done at all. I had to see him and explain how you'd helped me and what I had gleaned from you about your father. I wanted to remind him of how his own father was always doing just such things, yet what a splendid father he was and what a good husband and honest man. So I just "lit out" as Tom would say, leaving you to think all sorts of things, but hoping you'd believe in me.

I couldn't write before because, of course, Tom had to make a few inquiries; but they were satisfactory, just as I knew they would be, and now he'll take this with him when he goes to see your father.

Here's your lucky piece, my dear—the same one. I

found my purse tucked inside my waist when I went to bed. I knew I wasn't fit to travel by myself! Next time I go on a journey, I'll have to take you with me.

You can't think, dear child, how glad I am to know that you'll be going back to college after all and that I've been able, ever so indirectly, to play the part of your fairy godmother.

There was a moment's silence as Kathleen laid down the letter; and then she cried, "You don't mean, Dad, that my old lady's son Tom—"

"Oh, yes, I do!" interrupted Dad joyfully. "The business is saved, and I am on a salary—a salary that'll send you back to college. If you knew how it just broke my heart and Mother's to have you give it up—"

Dad stopped a moment to swallow, then went on. "Son Tom is all right! He's president of the very concern I've wanted to get in touch with. I tell you, Daughter, that *was* a lucky piece, wasn't it?"

"Why, Mother's crying!" exclaimed David suddenly.

"No, I'm not," contradicted Mother, although she dashed a telltale handkerchief across her eyes. "But you're mistaken this time, Father." She rose and, coming around the table, slipped between Kathleen and her father, putting an arm on each. "It wasn't the lucky piece at all," she said tenderly. "It was just the dear way you both have of believing the best of everyone."

And who would dare to say that Mother was not right?

The Snob

MORLEY CALLAGHAN

This is a disturbing story—a very disturbing story. So much so that when this collection was complete (I thought), the conviction came over me that there was something yet lacking, a missing dimension. And that missing dimension no story fills better than this one. It has to do with the receiving end of fatherhood, with the all-too-human tendency for children to regard fathers as back-numbers, perhaps even individuals we are secretly a bit ashamed of.

What if that secret shame were revealed to the father? Well, in such a case, you would have a story like "The Snob"—once read, virtually impossible to forget.

IT was at the book counter in the department store that John Harcourt, the student, caught a glimpse of his father. At first he could not be sure in the crowd that pushed along the aisle, but there was something about the color of the back of the elderly man's neck, something about the faded felt hat that he knew very well. Harcourt was standing with the girl he loved, buying a book for her. All afternoon he had been talking to her, eagerly but with an anxious diffidence, as if there still remained in him an innocent wonder that she should be delighted to be with him. From underneath her wide-brimmed straw hat, her face, so fair and beautifully strong with its expression of cool independence, kept turning up to him and sometimes smiled at what he said. That was the way they always talked, never daring to show much full, strong feeling. Harcourt had just bought the book and had reached into his pocket for the money with a free, ready gesture to make it appear that he was accustomed to buying books for young ladies, when the white-haired man in the faded felt hat at the other end of the counter turned half toward him, and Harcourt knew he was standing only a few feet away from his father.

The young man's easy words trailed away and his voice became little more than a whisper, as if he were afraid that everyone in the store might recognize it. There was rising in him a dreadful uneasiness; something very precious that he wanted to hold seemed close to destruction. His father, standing at the end of the bargain counter, was planted squarely on his two feet, turning a book over thoughtfully in his hands. Then he took out his glasses from an old, worn leather case and adjusted them on the end of his nose, looking down over them at the book. His coat was thrown open, two buttons on his vest were undone, his gray hair was too long, and in his rather shabby clothes he looked very much like a workingman, a carpenter perhaps. Such a resentment rose in young Harcourt that he wanted to cry out bitterly, "Why does he dress as if he never owned a decent suit in his life? He doesn't care what the whole world thinks of him. He never did. I've told him a hundred times he ought to wear his good clothes when he goes out. Mother's told him the same thing. He just laughs. And now Grace may see him. Grace will meet him."

So young Harcourt stood still, with his head down, feeling that something very painful was impending. Once he looked anxiously at Grace, who had turned to the bargain counter. Among those people drifting aimlessly by with hot, red faces, getting in each other's way, using their elbows but keeping their faces detached and wooden, she looked tall and splendidly alone. She was so sure of herself, her relation to the people in the aisles, the clerks behind the counters, the books on the shelves, and everything around her. Still keeping his head down and moving close, he whispered uneasily, "Let's go and have tea somewhere, Grace."

"In a minute, dear," she said.

"Let's go now."

"In just a minute, dear," she repeated absently.

"There's not a breath of air in here. Let's go now."

"What makes you so impatient?"

"There's nothing but old books on that counter."

"There may be something here I've wanted all my life," she said, smiling at him brightly and not noticing the uneasiness in his face.

So Harcourt had to move slowly behind her, getting closer to his father all the time. He could feel the space that separated them narrowing. Once he looked up with a vague, sidelong glance. But his father, red-faced and happy, was still reading the book, only now there was a meditative expression on his face, as if something in the book had stirred him and he intended to stay there reading for some time.

Old Harcourt had lots of time to amuse himself because he was on a pension after working hard all his life. He had sent John to the University and he was eager to have him distinguish himself. Every night when John came home, whether it was early or late, he used to go into his father and mother's bedroom and turn on the light and talk to them about the interesting things that had happened to him during the day. They listened and shared this new world with him. They both sat up in their nightclothes, and while his mother asked all the questions, his father listened attentively with his head cocked on one side and a smile or a frown on his face. The memory of all this was in John now, and there was also a desperate longing and a pain within him growing harder to bear as he glanced fearfully at his father, but he thought stubbornly, *I can't introduce him. It'll be easier for everybody if he doesn't see us. I'm not ashamed. But it will be easier. It'll be more sensible. It'll only embarrass him to see Grace.* By this time he knew he was ashamed, but he felt that his shame was justified, for Grace's father had the smooth, confident manner of a man who had lived all his life among people who were rich and sure of themselves. Often when he had been in Grace's home talking politely to her mother, John had kept on thinking of the plainness of his own home and of his parents' laughing, good-natured untidiness, and he resolved desperately that he must make Grace's people admire him.

He looked up cautiously, for they were about eight feet away from his father, but at that moment his father, too, looked up and John's glance shifted swiftly far over the aisle, over the counters, seeing nothing. As his father's blue, calm eyes stared steadily over the glasses, there was an instant when their glances might have met. Neither one could have been certain, yet John, as he turned away and began to talk hurriedly to Grace, knew surely that his father had seen him. He knew it by the steady calmness in his father's blue eyes. John's shame grew, and then humiliation sickened him as he waited and did nothing.

His father turned away, going down the aisle, walking erectly in his shabby clothes, his shoulders very straight, never once looking back. His father would walk slowly down the street, he knew, with that meditative expression deepening and becoming grave.

Young Harcourt stood beside Grace, brushing against her soft shoulder, and was made faintly aware again of the delicate scent she used. There, so close beside him, she was holding within her everything he wanted to reach out for, only now he felt a sharp hostility that made him sullen and silent. "You were right, John," she was drawling in her soft voice. "It does get unbearable in here on a hot day. Do let's go now. Have you ever noticed that department stores after a time can make you really hate people?" But she smiled when she spoke, so he might see that she really hated no one.

"You don't like people, do you?" he said sharply.

"People? What people? What do you mean?"

"I mean," he went on irritably, "you don't like the kind of people you bump into here, for example."

"Not especially. Who does? What are you talking about?"

"Anybody could see you don't," he said recklessly, full of a savage eagerness to hurt her. "I say you don't like simple, honest people, the kind of people you meet all over the city." He blurted the words out as if he wanted to shake her, but he was longing to say, "You wouldn't like my family. Why couldn't I take you home to have dinner with them? You'd turn up your nose at them because they've no pretensions. As soon as my father saw you, he knew you wouldn't want to meet him. I could tell by the way he turned."

His father was on his way home now, he knew, and that evening at dinner they would meet. His mother and

121

sister would talk rapidly, but his father would say nothing to him or to anyone. There would only be Harcourt's memory of the level look in the blue eyes and the knowledge of his father's pain as he walked away.

Grace watched John's gloomy face as they walked through the store, and she knew he was nursing some private rage, and so her own resentment and exasperation kept growing, and she said crisply, "You're entitled to your moods on a hot afternoon, I suppose, but if I feel I don't like it here, then I don't like it. You wanted to go yourself. Who likes to spend very much time in a department store on a hot afternoon? I begin to hate every stupid person that bangs into me, everybody near me. What does that make me?"

"It makes you a snob."

"So I'm a snob now?" she asked angrily.

"Certainly you're a snob," he said. They were at the door and going out to the street. As they walked into the sunlight in the crowd moving slowly down the street, he was groping for words to describe the secret thoughts he had always had about her. "I've always known how you'd feel about people I like who didn't fit into your private world," he said.

"You're a very stupid person," she said. Her face was flushed now, and it was hard for her to express her indignation, so she stared straight ahead as he walked along.

They had never talked in this way, and now they were both quickly eager to hurt each other. With a flow of words, she started to argue with him, then she checked herself and said calmly, "Listen, John, I imagine you're tired of my company. There's no sense in having tea together. I think I'd better leave you right here."

"That's fine," he said. "Good afternoon."

"Good-bye."

"Good-bye."

She started to go; she had gone two paces, but he reached out desperately and held her arm, and he was frightened and pleading. "Please don't go, Grace."

All the anger and irritation had left him; there was just a desperate anxiety in his voice as he pleaded, "Please forgive me. I've no right to talk to you like that. I don't know why I'm so rude or what's the matter. I'm ridiculous. I'm very, very ridiculous. Please, you must forgive me. Don't leave me."

He had never talked to her so brokenly, and his sincerity, the depth of his feeling, began to stir her. While she listened, feeling all the yearning in him, they seemed to have been brought closer together, by opposing each other, than ever before, and she began to feel almost shy. "I don't know what's the matter. I suppose we're both irritable. It must be the weather," she said. "But I'm not angry, John."

He nodded his head miserably. He longed to tell her that he was sure she would have been charming to his father, but he had never felt so wretched in his life. He held her arm tight, as if he must hold it or what he wanted most in the world would slip away from him, yet he kept thinking, as he would ever think, of his father walking away quietly with his head never turning.

The Hidden Talent

D. B. MURPHY JR.

Charles was positive his father was wrong: of course his classmates would ridicule him, would laugh at him, wouldn't have the slightest interest in his music.

But Dad didn't back down.

Well, he'd just have to prove him wrong—that's what he'd do.

WITH his hands in his pockets, he sauntered through the rambling garden, halfheartedly whistling some disjointed air. A vagrant breeze tousled his curly hair as his serious gray eyes sought his favorite nook. On reaching the secluded spot, he disdained the stone garden seat and flung himself on the grass.

Through the grove of tall poplars, he could look down and see the dappled river napping in the late afternoon sun. This was a pleasant place. Often he had come here to be alone, to read, to practice. The only intruders were the little clouds that sometimes peeped inquisitively over the poplars then fled away pell-mell. A faraway thrush sang ecstatically in the waning light, and the leaves of the poplars trembled timidly at the whisperings of the wind.

The dreaming boy did not hear the footsteps of his father in the clipped grass. Only after the kindly doctor had seated himself beside his preoccupied son and spoken his name did he start from his reverie.

"Charles," he said softly. The boy sat erect and looked a bit sheepish. "Don't bother to get up; I think I'll join you." So the two, father and son, lay side by side and gazed up at the wandering clouds already tinged with sunset gold.

Dr. Wilson had long wished for such an opportunity as this to discuss with his son something that was weighing heavily upon his heart. And yet he hardly knew how to begin. Where was all his efficiency? Now, if ever, he must summon all his powers of persuasion, logic, and rhetoric to unlock the treasure that lay buried in the soul of his seventeen-year-old son. It was going to be a battle.

"Charles, I hear that the young people are giving a musical program next Wednesday night, the proceeds of which are to be given to the Red Cross."

Charles's face darkened, but he said nothing.

"I'm sorry you declined to play, Son, but I've taken the liberty to tell them that you will reconsider. I don't wish to be harsh with you, but the time has long since passed when you should have learned that a musician's talents are not given him solely for his personal amusement."

Charles was so taken by surprise that at first he could only stare at his father in amazement. "But, Dad," he exclaimed, "they don't care for my kind of music—for classical music. They feed on that cheap trash that's here today and gone tomorrow."

"That may be true, but how much have *you* done to help to change their tastes? You may condemn their bad music, but what efforts have you made to show them that classical music is vastly superior? You, whom God has blessed with a marvelous talent, are burying that talent."

Charles winced at this accusation; he did have a conscience. Yet he still rebelled at the idea of baring his soul to the candid eye of the public. He reveled in his music. He lived and breathed it. Was it not his own secret treasure, to be securely locked away and brought out only when it pleased *him?* It always had been. Perhaps, though, his father was right about burying his talent, but he knew he was right about defending the classics. He would like to show his friends how really glorious the best music is. They had never heard him play. They all knew that he spent much time with his "fiddle" as they called it, but his persistent reluctance to play in public had almost frozen their interest in his accomplishment.

Father and son discussed the matter further for the next hour, and finally Charles yielded. Yes, he would play.

"I'm glad," his father said, rising slowly. "I knew that if you really loved your art, sooner or later you would come to its defense. I wish you would play 'The Maid with the Flaxen Hair' by Debussy. Promise?"

Charles said nothing; he was gazing absently at the evening star already glittering like a diamond on the blue velvet of the soft summer sky. Dr. Wilson turned quietly and went back to the house, inwardly elated that he had won such a signal victory. Charles remained on the grass only a little while longer; then he rose and followed his father.

That evening after supper Mrs. Wilson sat down at the piano, and Charles picked up his violin for their customary hour of music. With a wise smile she chose the Debussy selection first. Charles glanced quickly at his father, but encountered only a wide expanse of newspaper. With a smile and a half sigh, he tucked his violin under his chin and began. The intangible perfection of the music pervaded the room like an exquisite perfume.

"That was lovely, dear," she said softly at the end.

"Yes, but I know I can't do it that well on the program."

"But you will; you must," she assured him, rising and placing her long, white fingers on her young son's frowning forehead.

Charles grew increasingly nervous as the week passed. He had often played for a small circle of adult musicians of the city, but he had never played for his school associates. His father said nothing more. The day approached. What would his classmates think of him after next Wednesday night?

They drove to the school auditorium a little late that eventful evening. Charles had his violin case beside him on the backseat, and his music portfolio was on the floor. The long line of parked cars and the brightly lighted auditorium gave him a thrill that was somehow pleasant and unpleasant at the same time.

As they walked into the crowded room, the chatter of his schoolmates made him forget his uneasiness. Dr. Wilson found a seat in the anteroom adjoining the stage, reserved for the participants in the program. There, among assorted accordions, cornets, and excited sopranos, they found a place to sit.

The master of ceremonies, a bustling young man with red hair, asked whether they were all ready. He then stepped briskly onto the stage, and the program was on.

The first number was a mournful saxophone solo played by a sleepy-looking youth whose nasal honks seemed to please the audience greatly. Charles did not listen to the following selections. He simply endured them. There were some accordion duets, a trombone solo, one or two fairly good vocal solos; but on the whole, the program was not high class, to say the least. Yet that audience seemed to enjoy it.

Nudging his mother, he said, "I told you they would not like my music." She said nothing but smiled encouragingly.

"Ladies and gentlemen, we have a special treat this evening. Charles Wilson, a talented young violinist of our neighborhood, has consented to play for us. We appreciate his presence, and I know we shall enjoy his music. He will play Debussy's 'The Maid with the Flaxen Hair.' His mother will accompany him."

There followed a faint applause.

Mrs. Wilson sat down at the piano. Charles tuned his violin, and then he was ready to begin. But he paused a moment. It was hard to start when there was so much rustling and loud whispering. His very demeanor soon quieted the audience. Nodding to his mother, he fastened his eyes on the farthest corner and began to play.

He drew the notes like magic bubbles from off the strings and lightly flung them out over the upturned faces of the listeners. Enchanted, the audience hardly dared to breathe. Here was something new, something beautiful, something fragile. Yet with all its fragility, it was enduring, uplifting, and refreshing.

The piece was short; yet the spell was not broken until Charles had made his bow and stepped off the stage. Then a tumult of applause shook the auditorium.

There was a lump in Dr. Wilson's throat. Indeed there were lumps in many throats. The simple, appealing message played straight from the boy's heart had done its work.

After the program Charles was surprised when many shook his hand and thanked him profusely for his part of the program. His classmates were especially complimentary, and their praise he valued the most. Perhaps his effort had not been in vain. He sincerely hoped that he had raised the classics in the estimation of at least some of the young moderns who were his high school friends. And although he felt unusually happy, he did not realize what the program had done for him.

His father said little on the way home. His mother assured him that he had never played better, but besides that she said little. Inwardly she was tremendously thrilled, but she knew that gushing praise, though sincere, would be unwise. Charles was too relieved and tired to say much.

The next evening after supper, Dr. Wilson called him into the library. "Sit down, Son; I want to talk to you."

Charles took the leather chair facing his father's desk.

"Have you discovered my real purpose in insisting that you play last night?" he began with a twinkle in his eye.

Charles glanced quizzically at his father. "What do you mean?"

"I mean that the program last night drew you out of the shell in which you have long taken refuge. You revolved in your own little orbit, engrossed in your music, not caring for other companionship. You excused yourself by saying that your associates did not care for the music you enjoyed. But you found out last night that they appreciated your playing more than any other part of the program. That pleased you. And now you are ready to share your music freely, to give pleasure to others, and not to remain so self-centered. That is as it should be, and I am pleased."

An hour later the kindly old moon made the garden a study in black and white. From the stone seat Charles could hear the murmur of the river beyond the poplars. The cool night air fanned his face and whispered many things in his ear.

Yes, dear old dad had been right. He *did* feel unusually contented and pleased. He *did* feel as though he had been released from a shell. If the old moon had bent a little closer, it could have seen many things in Charles's gray eyes: lofty ideals, determination, and, above all, a noble answer to the call of service.

The river murmured and sang as it hastened on to blend its waters with the waters of the sea.

Who Said Rats?

LEWIS CAVINESS

In one respect, Father was still a boy who had never grown up. Both his daughters and long-suffering wife knew the signs all too well. The signs that he was entering a new stage, a new involvement, a new hobby, a new obsession.

And now . . . could it possibly be . . . rats?

MOTHER! Mother! Just listen to this!" Father began a walk through the house toward the kitchen, reading his paper as he went and bumping into all the furniture on the way. But then, it didn't hurt Father any; Father was fat.

"Mother, listen to this, now! Where are you? In the pantry? Oh, all right. Now notice!

"'Considerable interest is being manifested these days in Sam Cardia's window, where a family of white mice is on exhibition. There seems to be quite a market for these rodents at present. During the war they were found to be valuable in being especially susceptible to the effects of poisonous gas. Since then they are being used in laboratory experiments where rabbits were formerly used. White

mice seem most adaptable to experimental purposes since they are hardy, require less care and food than rabbits, and breed more rapidly. Probably many people will undertake the breeding of these little animals as a remunerative pastime. They are interesting creatures and often show marked sagacity.'"

Mother had stopped her work, the spoon still in her uplifted hand. When he had finished, she looked him all over with her twinkling gray eyes. She knew Father.

"Well?"

"Now wait a minute till I find that other item. Yes, here it is, under 'Pets and Poultry.' 'White Mice— breed rapidly and require little care. Information furnished as to food and housing. Two pair for $10. Guarantee to purchase at fair price all animals produced. Sam Cardia, 4th Street and Cottonwood Avenue.'"

"Now isn't that interesting?" Father ran his fingers through his hair until it stood up straight in front.

"Why shouldn't I get a quartet of those rascals? They wouldn't take any time. I could care for them mornings when I look after the furnace. And they are prolific, you know. Little expense and no bother to anybody. That's the talk. I shall begin with one or two pair. I—I think it's a capital idea!"

Mother was cutting her cake. It required attention, but there was a look in her eye and a straight line along her back that had nothing whatever to do with cutting the cake.

"I know you do, dear," she said. "You always do."

127

"Well, what's the matter with it? I'd like to know. That's the difficulty of being one man in a houseful of strong-minded women—even if they are my own wife and daughters. They never give a man liberty to try out his own ideas. Talk about freedom of the will!"

"Father!"

"Oh, all right! I shan't try it if you are set against it; but for the life of me I can't see why I shouldn't."

"Call the girls, Father, won't you? We are all ready for supper."

The girls came and they sat down, Father silent and apparently perfectly harmless; though Mother, being long used to his conflagrations, knew he was only smoldering and might break out in a new place any minute.

Just as they were finishing the meal, Father looked up from under his bushy eyebrows, laughing and folding his hands cherublike, and asked meekly, "Mother, may I please go to the library? I've a new book I want to be at."

His meekness and the chuckle in his voice set them all laughing, and of course explanations had to follow. Father was not naturally so meek at all.

"But Daddy, you wouldn't really do it, would you? Not *rats!*"

You'd have thought the rats were already under their feet to hear the girls' protests.

"Why not, I'd like to know? They'd be in the basement, and nobody need know, if you're so particular. Though Hinkley has a whole cellar of quad-

rupeds for his laboratory! Why shouldn't I have two pair of white mice with pink eyes? Color combination's all right, isn't it?"

"But Father!"—both girls at once this time, and Mother stopped laughing suddenly and sat up very straight.

"Allen Reed Washburn!" Father fled to the library, calling back that he would surrender.

When he had gone, Mother and the girls laughed until they cried. Father knew they would; then they sobered down and got to business. Talk about "Bringing Up Father!" That task was nothing to theirs. They had to forever keep settling Father down. The council closed as it often had before.

"Mumsie, you don't really think he'll do it, do you? Why the things smell, don't they? And people would be horrified. We couldn't have people know it. He won't do it surely, will he?"

"I hope not, girls. But I can't say. Father's hypnotized with printer's ink. If he reads something, it's so. Part of Father never grew up, that's all. You know how it has always been. Once it was Alberta. Once it was fancy chickens; and when those two prize cocks killed each other fighting, it was spineless cactus; next it was milch goats; and now I'm afraid it's going to be white mice. If he were only as conservative about his hobbies as he is about psychology; but he isn't—he never is. We'll just have to hope he forgets about it."

As a matter of fact, it turned out that Mother forgot about it—Mother and the girls.

A week later, Mother opened the cellar door one afternoon just in time to surprise Father indulging in a beautific smile. She looked at him a full minute and then—remembering—asked severely, "Well, Father, where are they?" She started downstairs to see for herself. The white rats had come!

"Oh, Mother, go back upstairs. There's nothing for you to worry over down here! What's got hold of you? The furnace is all right."

But Mother was marching straight ahead, following her nose, and evidently her nose had a way of knowing where to go. Away at the back, near the outside door, she found them, in an abandoned chick

brooder—four frightened, long-tailed, pink-eyed white rats! Father stood behind her sheepishly and heaved a sigh of unmistakable relief. Double life would have been a strain on Father. It was easier now that Mother knew.

Just then Mother turned around. Her face was grim. "Now you think you've done it, don't you?" she said. The corners of Father's mouth twitched as if he wanted to laugh and didn't dare. Mother went on:

"But you will regret this. Mark my word. Those rats will be all over this house. Don't say they can't get out of the box. They'll be into my linen closet, and into the girls' dresser drawers, and into your manuscripts! See if they don't! However, it's done; we'll say as little as possible about it; only don't go bringing people down here to see them."

Mother turned and marched upstairs, looking for all the world as she did when she went to the faculty reception in her best gray satin—she was that grand—and Father fed his pets and followed her discreetly.

The girls were privately advised as to the arrival of Father's rats and requested to avoid discussion of the whole matter.

All went well.

The rodents in the Washburn basement waxed fat. They were fruitful; they multiplied and made some progress toward replenishing the earth. Father fed them faithfully, and Mother and girls tried hard to ignore their existence.

However, one morning Mrs. Davis, the thrifty neighbor from over the way, stopped in to inquire as to the innards of the Washburn furnace, the Davis furnace having developed a temperament to the extent that the plumber maintained it would have to be replaced.

"Mine's downdraft," Father said, getting up from his desk and sending the papers over the floor in a swirl as he came out of the library, hearing Mrs. Davis's questions. "Works fine. I've had it in six years without a repair. Want to see it? Come down."

Blind to the menacing flare in Mother's eyes, he led the way to the regions below for Mrs. Davis to inspect the furnace. Mother followed the two—not because she wanted to, but because she might be needed. Father was not so quick on the comeback as he might be.

Midway in the animated description of the superior points of the downdraft, Mrs. Davis lifted her head and sniffed. Suddenly her already sharp nose and chin became sharper.

"Mrs. Washburn, I smell mice in your cellar! I'd never believe it of as good a housekeeper as you; but I do. You ought to have a cat. Don't you smell mice, Mrs. Washburn? Don't you now?"

Mother's face—if it could have been scrutinized in the dim light of the basement—looked as guilty as the time-honored child caught in the pantry with jam on his face, but she only said, "There were none a month ago, I know. I'll have to look around tomorrow and see."

The furnace was forgotten. Mrs. Davis had discovered a possible delinquency in her neighbor's housekeeping. What was a description of furnace types to this? With diplomacy she was restrained from searching the cellar herself. They finally got her upstairs, still insisting that something surely smelled like mice anyway. And when she was gone, Father fairly fled into his study and shut the door to escape the consequences. . . .

"I may be late for dinner tonight, Mother," the head of the Psychology Department said as he buttoned up his overcoat one afternoon. "This is faculty meeting day, you know. I'll feed the furnace, so you won't need to think of it. Good-bye everybody!" he called back as he went down to the cellar. The rat family was flattering in its welcome and fell upon the corn. "Now that's all for tonight. Let's see, that door is loose; must mend that tomorrow. There! Did one of those rascals get out? Don't see him anywhere. Was mistaken! Must hurry now."

Up the backstairs he tramped, across the lawn—crocuses were coming on fine—two blocks down to the campus and in among the fine trees to the administration building. Several of his fellow professors joined him on the way up. The head of the Psychology Department loved it all, loved the quiet of the little college town that dozed about the campus, loved the traditions of the institution. He was ruminating over this as he came into the council room. The President was bending over his papers before them; groups of instructors and professors visited in undertones about the room. Dr. Washburn found his place in one group and fell into conversation.

"Now the advantages of experimental psychology over the old class lecture method are obvious," he was soon saying. He took off his glasses and began going through his pockets in his usual systematic search for a handkerchief. "The laboratory is the modern means of acquiring knowledge. Psychology is one of the last branches of the curriculum to take it up." *Must be in the other pocket.* "And we have been slow to advance. Next year we must foster it, introduce a minor course—"

What in the world? Why, something warm and furry and cold and scratchy and wiggly all at once! The head of the Department of Psychology rose suddenly and precipitately out of his seat! There was a squeal, a flash of white across the room in the direction of a group of women instructors! Men shouted with laughter! Women screamed; some climbed onto chairs! One jerked off a slipper and made for the rat; everybody jumped up and gave chase! Chairs tipped over; people ran every which way and pounded the floor and each other's feet assiduously! Presently the hunted beast found a crack under the door large enough to squeeze through and vanished. By degrees the excitement and hilarity in the faculty room subsided, and the day's business was more or less seriously attacked. But the head of the Department of Psychology was missing. One might have seen him—if one had looked— nearly running down the street for home.

"Mother!" he panted as he stumbled up the front steps.

"Mother!" And he banged open the door and grabbed the telephone receiver. "Mother! What's— Cardia's phone number? Quick!" Mother came hurrying from the living room where she was receiving callers.

"Get me Cardia's number, won't you? Oh, what difference does it make? Hurry! Those pesky rats. Here, give it to me! Oh, you *have* to have it! Oh, hello, hello, Black 3238. Yes. That you, Sam? This is Washburn. Got some white rats for you! Can you come for them today? . . . Yes, this afternoon . . . No, not to-morrow—*tonight!* . . . Send a boy today . . . No, I'll not help catch them. You'll take the whole box! . . . How do I know how many there are? Will you come and get them, I say? . . . Oh, all right. Good-bye!"

After dinner, a more than ordinarily quiet dinner during which no one dared even say "rats," Father was reading his paper, and Mother was crocheting. Presently Father kicked over the footstool and stood up.

"There, Mother," he said, "just listen to this. Here's the very washing machine I've always wanted you to have. Different than any you ever saw. It's simple as can be, too. The principle is the thing. Now listen." Father looked up to see if Mother was listening, and he saw something in her face that made him throw back his head and laugh till the tears ran down his cheeks. Mother laughed, too, and the advertisement section of the evening news fell harmlessly on the library floor. Father was cured of rats. Perhaps he was cured of other hobbies as well. Perhaps not!

The Window Tree

JOAN MARIE COOK

*No matter how much an adopted child loves his or her
adoptive parents, deep down there will always be
questions, a yearning to know who the biological parents
were, who the blood family was—the ancestry in its
broader sense.*

Not knowing leaves a piece of life's puzzle unresolved.

Within a wondrous little book (The Window Tree,
*published in 1960) is this brief story of a coed who loved
beauty—and who longed to meet, if only but once, her
father.*

My ROOM was undoubtedly the smallest
in the dormitory. The walls and an assortment of
pipes huddled together in a corner were painted an
exuberant pink that did something to one's nerves.
But there hadn't been many rooms left to choose
from, and something about this one endeared it to
me.

After supper as I was beginning to unpack my
trunk, a merry group of my neighbors swarmed into
my room. "We're touring the dorm to see all the
clever decorating schemes," one girl informed me,
"but since you're so slow, I suppose we'll have to visit
you later."

I liked this group of happy girls, I decided, as they
introduced themselves elaborately. One girl, who
proclaimed herself to be my next-door neighbor said,
"Did the dean make you take this room?"

"Well, no. You see, I didn't have one reserved, and
there weren't many left—"

"But there must be *something* else," another girl
said hopefully. "This is the very worst room in the
whole building. Maybe if you see the dean tonight
you can still change."

The other girls sympathetically pointed out the
room's all-too-obvious defects, but they laughed
when I said that I didn't plan to stay in my room
much anyway.

When the others were gone, Kelly, a quiet girl
with a fascinating crooked smile, stayed in my doorway. "I know your secret," she said, and her eyes were
wide with excitement. She reminded me of a small
child about to share a pleasant surprise. She snapped
off the light and crossed the room. "It's this wonderful window. That's what makes this room the best in
all the dormitory."

She stretched out her small, sturdy arms as if to
embrace what she saw. "Look at that. Just look."

I walked to the window, knowing what I would see.
A giant silver maple tree towered up to my window-
sill. It was planted several yards from the building, so
that looking down, one could see the whole perfect
tree. And in the moonlight, as now, it was a glorious

133

sight, with each gentle breeze changing every leaf into a shimmering, dancing illusion. Beyond the tree and across the campus one could always see the approach of the first evening star. When I sat or stood by the window and looked at the moonglow and the silver of the tree, a hushed feeling grew inside me, and it seemed I could think special thoughts.

Isn't it strange how, although there are many people we can talk with comfortably, there are only a few with whom we can share silence? I was amazed and pleased at Kelly's perception, but I did not need to speak and tell her so. We stood for a long while bathed in the beauty and calm and silence of the window. And we were friends ever after.

There was a certain vigor in Kelly's personality that gave a special charm to her otherwise plain looks. I can see her yet, sitting on the dormitory stairs after the room lights had been turned off, repeating and repeating a poem until she had it memorized—not as an assignment, but simply because she loved it.

Once Kelly told me of her life. She had been born in South America, where her father was a construction superintendent. Her parents were divorced when she was only a few months old. Her mother returned to America then, so Kelly never remembered seeing her real father.

"Not even a picture of him?" I asked incredulously.

"No. But he used to write to me some."

Her mother had remarried, and Kelly's new father had loved and adopted her. After a few years the family became converted, and in their new happiness no one would guess the unusual situation in the home. "I just want to *see* what my father is like," Kelly said. "Sometimes I get this strange feeling—almost a loneliness for him—even though I only know him through a few old letters. And I wonder, do you think he would love me?"

Kelly had a keen empathy with the elements. The window in her room was almost always flung open, so "we won't lose the majesty of the sunshine, the passion of the wind, or the sweetness of the rain," she often said, smiling. Walking with Kelly during a snowfall was an experience. She never trudged with her head bowed, clutching her coat to her as most do, but with her face lifted to meet the snowflakes. "Splendid, oh, how splendid!" she would say, dancing about with the wind. And the cold never seemed biting or ugly when she was there.

The day before Christmas vacation began we went on a happy shopping trip and returned to the dorm with icicles in our veins. I was halfway across the lobby when I heard a low, almost questioning voice speak Kelly's name.

Kelly was busy crossing our names off the monitor's checkout book. She turned, just as I did, to see who had spoken. The lobby was empty except for a tall man who stood by the fireplace. The deep tan of his face looked even darker in contrast to the steel gray of his hair. "Kelly," he said again, and no more.

Nothing moved in the swirling silence that surrounded us until Kelly spoke with no shade of uncertainty in her voice. "You are my father," she said.

And it was true.

I walked slowly up the stairs to my room. I stood at my window and thought for a long time. It seemed to me that the scene I had just witnessed was a great deal like some conversions. The sinner who has never known God hears one day a voice calling his name. And all the lonely one must do is turn about and say, "You are my Father."

Christmas Gift for Dad

MARY SHERMAN HILBERT

The telegram was delivered and nothing would ever be the same—Bob was killed in action somewhere on New Guinea in 1944. No one wanted to face Christmas that sad year, least of all Dad, who just sat there, staring stonily through the window.

Then, on December 23, another official package arrived . . . .

Mary Sherman Hilbert, a free-lance writer from Washington State, continues to write today. She is perhaps best known for her deeply moving, and oft-reprinted story, "A Sandpiper to Bring You Joy."

WE dreaded Christmas that year. It was 1944, and the war would never be over for our family.

The telegram had arrived in August. Bob's few personal possessions: the flag from his coffin, the plat of a burial site in the Philippine Islands, a Distinguished Flying Cross, had arrived one by one, adding to our misery.

Born on a Midwest prairie, my brother rode horseback to school but wanted to fly an airplane from the first day he saw one. By the time he was twenty-one, we were living in Seattle, Washington. When World War II broke out, Bob headed for the nearest Air Force recruitment office. Slightly built, skinny like his father, he was ten pounds underweight.

Undaunted, he persuaded Mother to cook every fattening food she could think of. He ate before meals, between meals, and after meals. We called him Fatso.

At the Navy Air Cadet office he stepped on the scales. Still three pounds to go. He was desperate. His friends were leaving one after the other, his best buddy already in the Marine Air Corps. He went home, ate ten bananas in a row, drank three gallons of milk, and, bloated like a pig, staggered back onto their scale. He passed the weigh-in with eight ounces to spare!

When he was nominated Hot Pilot of primary training school in Pasco, Washington, and involuntarily joined the Caterpillar Club (engine failure causing the bailout) at basic training in St. Mary's California, we shook our heads and worried. Mother prayed. He was born fearless and she knew it. Before graduating from Corpus Christi, he made application to transfer to the Marine Air Corps and was accepted. He was sent to Pensacola, Florida, and trained in torpedo bombers before being sent overseas.

They say Bob died under enemy fire over New Guinea in the plane he wanted so desperately to fly. . . .

I never wept for Bob. In my mind's eye I pictured my debonair brother "wing tapping" through the clouds—doing what he loved best, his blue eyes sparkling with love of life. But I wept for the sadness that never left my parents' eyes.

Mother's faith sustained her, but my father aged before our eyes. He would listen politely when the minister came to call, but we knew Daddy was bitter. He lost interest in everything, including his beloved Masonic Club. He stopped going to their meetings. Dad had always wanted a Masonic ring but felt it an unnecessary extravagance and never bought one.

Bob had always loved Christmas. His enthusiasm would excite us long before reason took over. His surprises were legendary: a dollhouse made at school, a puppy—hidden in mysterious places—for little brother, an expensive dress for Mother bought with the first money he ever earned. Everything had to be a surprise or it spoiled his fun.

What would Christmas be without Bob? Not much. Aunts, uncles, and Grandmother were coming so we went through the motions as much for memory as anything, but our hearts weren't in it. Dad sat for longer and longer periods, staring silently out the window. Mother prayed privately.

On December 23 another official-looking package arrived. My father watched stonefaced as Mother unpacked Bob's dress blues. Silence hung heavily. As she refolded the uniform to put away, a mother's practicality surfaced and she went through the pockets almost by rote, aching with grief.

In a small inside jacket pocket was a neatly folded fifty-dollar bill, with a tiny note in Bob's familiar handwriting: "For Dad's Masonic ring."

Mother cried out in amazement, and her eyes teared with pleading as she handed it to Daddy. We held our breaths. Would this be the straw that would completely break his heart?

If I live to be one hundred, I will never forget the look in my father's face. Some kind of beautiful transformation took place—a touch of wonder, a mite of joy. Oh, the healing power of love! He stood transfixed, then walked to Bob's picture hanging prominently on the wall and solemnly saluted.

"Merry Christmas, Son," he murmured. And turned to welcome Christmas.

There's a Wideness . . .

JOSEPH LEININGER WHEELER

A power other than God has taken control of this world's media and advertising, persuading us that financial success is more important than a personal relationship with our God. This subversive message so saturates the airwaves that it is almost impossible to remain unaffected by it.

Even Charles Huntington. And he already had it all.

CHARLES HUNTINGTON quietly stepped into his father's opulent study. At the far end of the long table, intently studying a near-mint first edition of Tolstoy's *Resurrection*, was a tall, distinguished-looking man with a mane of black hair (ever so faintly beginning to tinge with gray).

Since his entry hadn't been noticed, Charles's gaze wandered idly over the room. To his immediate left was a Caravaggio, the light from the fading sun giving it an almost unearthly luminosity. Across from it was one of the finest Georges de la Tour paintings in America. Just beyond the Louis XV desk were eight original sketches by Rembrandt. About thirty feet farther down that side of the room, highlighted by special lighting in a secured case, were three of Leonardo's inimitable horse sketches.

Rising symmetrically between the gothic columns were rows of oak, yew, and rosewood bookcases. On the shelves were books and manuscripts by the thousand. Softly, Charles edged over to the almost complete collection of Dickens in original serial wrappers. . . . Softening the sounds of his footsteps was one of the largest Esfahan carpets on the East Coast, dating back to the sixteenth century.

Just behind his father was a magnificent fireplace which had been carefully and tenderly dismantled, each part numbered, boxed, and moved out of a tottering seventeenth-century French chateau, transported by barge to Marseilles, by ship to Baltimore, and thence by barge down the Chesapeake Bay to Annapolis, then up the Severn River to Round Bay, there to be reassembled on one of the largest tracts of land in urban Maryland.

Logs were crackling and spitting, and the flames cast a cheery glow over his father in his battered old chair. Many times Mother had threatened to haul the atrocity out, but her husband, who humored his beautiful wife most of the time, was, in this case, as unyielding as the rocky cliffs of Acadia. He cared not a whit if it *did* jar the harmony of the great study; it was the most comfortable chair he had ever found—so there it stayed. Speaking of Mother, above Marshall

Huntington's massive desk, just to the left of the dramatic cobalt blue window (Tiffany's transformation into glass of Maxfield Parrish's "Dawn") hung a more modern painting, this one depicting a nineteen-year-old Hapsburg princess . . . three years before her marriage to Marshall Huntington, one of the richest men in the world and related to half the royal houses in Europe.

Purring contentedly on his father's lap was Genghis Khan. Genghis, a veteran of many a Baltimore ghetto street battle, had casually sauntered onto the estate grounds one nippy fall day, slipped by the guards and house security personnel, and then wandered into the study, sized up the senior Huntington, leaped onto his lap, contentedly relaxed, and began to groom his battle-scarred fur coat, to the continual litany of the loudest purr Huntington had ever heard. . . . So total was his domination of the library and all who ventured within, that Charles's cousin, Natasha, then a precocious nine-year-old, after having seen a rather violent historical movie in the screening room one afternoon, declared that the tomcat was every bit as supreme in his kingdom as was Genghis Khan in *his*. The name stuck. . . . Even the butlers, attendants, and guards walked softly in his presence.

Shattering the evening's quietness were the staccato sounds of galloping hooves, gradually becoming louder. Charles smiled fondly as an older Natasha thundered up the drive. The lovely fourteen-year-old was about as horse crazy as a human can get.

No sooner had Natasha dismounted, turned the horse over to a groom, and slammed the east porch door, than a much quieter sound—a low smooth hum, punctuated only by ricocheting gravel—announced the arrival of Robert's 1934 Silver Ghost. . . . Higgins, one of the doormen, hastened to the car and opened the rear door. Uncoiling himself, dressed in an immaculate gray suit, was twenty-four-year-old Robert Franz Joseph Huntington, so unbearably proper and self-righteous that Charles devoutly hoped his elder brother would somehow rip his suit getting out of his Rolls. . . . But no such luck!

Robert's regal arrival jarred Charles out of his reverie and reminded him of his mission, so he cleared his throat and strode across the long room to his father.

The older man looked up to see his strikingly handsome twenty-one-year-old son walking quickly toward him. Within his mind, pain battled with pleasure and pride, for his relationship with headstrong Charles had been rockier than ever during the last few weeks and months. Charles had been expelled from Yale about a month earlier: a number of scrapes, culminating with a police raid which uncovered a large stash of marijuana, opium, and heroin in Charles's living quarters, finally resulted in the university president regretfully phoning his old friend and classmate, Marshall, telling him that matters had now gone too far.

Ever since Charles's untimely return from Yale, the father had known that a showdown was imminent. He could not condone the reckless and abandoned lifestyle the young man seemed determined to live. Since his return, Charles had given every indication that he had given up on securing a university degree, had done little to help in the administration of the worldwide interests of the Huntingtons, and was drinking more and more openly. How this degeneration hurt the father, for the young man had rare potential, had always been able to charm people—his parents included—and thus avoid the natural consequences of his continual scrapes. The father sighed and mused to himself that he had probably been too easy on him. As for his mother, ever since his first impish baby grin demolished her maternal walls, she had been his slave. Robert, of course, quickly noticed this obvious partiality—and deeply resented it.

"Father!" So unnaturally tense and high-pitched was the voice that Marshall froze his wandering thoughts. "Father . . . I want out! . . . I'm sick of the academic rat race. . . . I'm sick of this country . . . this state . . . this city . . . this house . . . and *this family!* . . . They're *such* a bore. . . . Let Robert play with them— the old apple-polisher. *Robert* won't do anything wrong. . . . *He'll* never rock the family boat!"

"*Charles!*" What pain scarred the voice—pain that was completely ignored by the young man.

"I mean it, Father! . . . No, please hear me out! . . . I've thought about it for weeks now. . . . I'm *through.* . . . Not being a hypocrite, I'm going to say it straight. . . . I want to leave this place and never return here again! . . . I want to live life in the fast lane. . . . Why wait until I am gray-headed? . . . Gusto . . . that's what I want; only *fools* postpone gusto. . . . Father . . . I . . . I . . . I want . . . what's . . . uh . . . what's . . . uh . . . coming to me *now.*"

"Charles!! Just what do you mean? Surely . . . you don't mean . . ."

"I surely *do!* . . . OK . . . your will, Father . . . If you and Mother were to be killed in an accident—such things *do* happen, you know—what . . . uh . . . percentage would I get?"

"Percentage? . . . Oh . . . uh . . . half, I should guess."

"That's what I thought. Well, I want my half *now!* No Puritan work ethic for me. I'm going to enjoy it *now.* . . . Why, Father, you have so much money I couldn't spend half of it in a lifetime if I worked at it full-time for a *hundred years!*"

"You want to liquidate *half* of what we own . . . *today!* . . . How? . . . We'd lose a lot by this kind of forced liquidation . . . besides, it would take time."

"Oh, I'll be reasonable. . . . I know about what you and Mother are worth. . . . Robert and I have discussed it. . . . Altogether, you are worth somewhere between 4 and 5 billion dollars . . . and that's not even counting the Rothschild inheritance, which can't be broken up . . . but I'm not greedy. I'll settle for 2 billion."

"*Two billion!*"

"Yeah . . . don't look at me like that! I read the papers; you just sold your GM stock for $650 million. You always keep cash reserves of at least $500 million. My attorney has spelled it all out." He pulled a crumpled sheet of paper out of his back pocket. "Here it is; it's all in this document . . . it won't have to come all at once. As I said, I'm reasonable . . . $500 million to be credited to my account with our bank in Zurich . . . within thirty days from now, and the remaining billion and a half in installments of $500 million during each of the next three years. . . . Here, it's all in this document!"

"*So* . . . so Perkins drew this up for you . . . hmm . . . looks to be in order . . . but Charles . . . are you *sure* this is what you really want?"

"*Of course I am!* . . . Father, I just want to get out . . . for good! . . . I'm just a bad egg—and you don't know yet just *how* bad . . . but *you will!* . . . But you'll have Robert to comfort you—good ol' Robert." And here Charles cackled in a most unpleasant manner.

Marshall recoiled as though seared by a sizzling brand.

"Good riddance . . . eh . . . Father? Couple of billion to get rid of me for life? . . . And you'll *never* see me again! That's a promise. . . . I say it's a darn good bargain."

"But Charles . . . we *want* to see you . . . we *love*—"

"Aw, cut it, Father . . . that's for the galleries. . . . Love . . . that's a laugh. It's fake. This whole world is fake. . . . *All* . . . except for money. Now *that's* real! . . . Will you sign, Father?"

"Well . . . yes . . . as soon as our attorneys check out the logistics. It'll mean selling off corporations that have been owned by the family for genera-tions—what a *shock* that will be . . . a lot of jobs are likely to be lost. How can I face these people who have placed their trust in me . . . who have dedicated their *lives* to our service?"

"Welcome to the real world, Father. . . . That's the way things work in business: dog eat dog. Sounds good enough for me. We can just shake on it: The whole world knows your handshake is more binding than a ton of legal print. Shake hands, Father?"

"All right . . . as you wish, Charles." His voice broke.

"Good! Tell Mother I'm sorry I missed her . . . when she gets back from St. Moritz. As for Robert, now he can rule the heir apparent's roost alone, for all he's worth. . . . Now, don't be gettin' all misty eyed, Father. You just made one of the best bargains of your life. This is good-bye, Father. . . . Some things are just not meant to be. . . . *You will never see me again.*"

Minutes later, the red Maserati sped down the long driveway, by the gatekeeper, and screamed out of sight.

And . . . in the study, several hours later, when Hesseltine came in with the evening coffee and cakes, he found the fire reduced to embers . . . and his employer with his face buried in his hands.

FLOODTIDE

For Charles, the years fled by on the eagle-swift wings of pleasure and debauchery. He spent $150 million on a floating palace, *Midsummer Night's*

Dream, which carried him and his companions back and forth across the globe. When he wanted to move more quickly, they shuttled on one of his private jets—Paris yesterday, Rome today, Bangkok tomorrow.

He became legendary at the casinos, winning . . . and losing . . . with flair. In one night at Monte Carlo, he dropped $5 million.

Liquor . . . drugs . . . and beautiful women.

The Bahamas . . . Rio . . . Buenos Aires . . . Capetown . . . Nairobi . . . Stockholm . . . Nice . . . Vienna . . . Leningrad . . . Salzburg . . . St. Moritz . . . London . . . Hong Kong . . . Singapore . . . Tokyo . . . Melbourne . . . Tahiti . . . Naples . . .

He raced at Le Mans . . . he hunted elephants in Kenya . . . he played polo in New Zealand . . . he scuba dived off Capri . . . he consulted with seers in Hindustan . . . he matched wits with Arab sheiks in Damascus . . . his caravans inched across the top of the world in Nepal and Tibet . . . he sauntered into La Scala . . . dead drunk . . . and caused such a scene that he was thrown into the street.

"No commitment" was his motto, thus his life was one long succession of one-night stands, only a few lasting a week or more.

Only at rare intervals—usually when recovering from a long period of debauchery—did he ever think of Father and of home . . . but never for more than a few minutes, for his good-time companions always kept the action in high gear. As a result, slivers of silence in which he could actually think and reflect grew increasingly rare as the years whirled past.

Known everywhere for his free-spending ways, he was always surrounded by "friends" who continually told him how wonderful he was. Hundred-dollar tips ensured him the best tables and service everywhere. In the world's most elite hotels, he commonly leased entire floors for his entourage. As for insurance and other bookkeeping bothers . . . who cared! For his treasure chest was inexhaustible.

As his whim dictated, he was likely to buy castles in Spain, chateaus in France, monasteries in Mexico, palaces in Germany, islands in Greece, apartment houses in Hamburg, ranches in the Australian Outback or the Argentine pampas, tea estates in India, and banks in Beirut.

In the Western world, his name was as well known as the names of ruling princes and presidents: Tabloid pulp magazines and society columns listed his comings and goings—with star billing—along with Prince Charles, Princess Grace, Elizabeth Taylor, Cary Grant, Aristotle Onassis and the reigning sports and media superstars of the day. Truly, the world was his.

THE FALL

But it is a long road which has no turning. It was one of those pea-soup nights the English Channel is famous for. The *Midsummer Night's Dream* had seen some wild parties through the years, but none as unrestrained as this one. Even the pilot had succumbed to the mood of the orgy; thus there was no one at the helm.

Just off the coast of Dover, there was the sound of screaming metal followed by a horrible shudder . . . and the palatial yacht, within minutes, began to list as water flooded into the hull. The ship began to sink. So inebriated were the guests and crew that the lifeboats were forgotten as they leaped overboard. Since they were so close to land, a little over half of them (including Charles) made it to shore; some, immobilized by liquor, sank with the ship, and the others drowned attempting to get to shore.

The media spotlight, Janus-like, covered the tragedy to its fullest, then tiring of the years of litigation which followed, turned elsewhere for their stories. The erstwhile friends who survived and the heirs of those who did not sued Charles for gross negligence—and collected to the tune of several hundred million dollars. And he had no insurance—had laughed at ever needing any. For over five years, he was in the courts almost continually; with each judgment, yet another of his assets had to be sold—often at a heavy loss—in order to pay it.

Reeling from these judgments against him but still confident that he could weather the storm, he was racked—as was all Europe—when the President of the Swiss bank where he kept the bulk of his reserves absconded with over $3 billion and fled—rumor had it—to somewhere in South America. There was, as a result, a massive run on the bank. Within forty-eight hours, it closed its doors, never to reopen.

Almost frantic by now, Charles sold his remaining properties one by one; some, which were slow to sell, were repossessed because of his inability to keep up with the taxes. For yet another year, he was able to hold out. Then when a London jury awarded the largest yet maritime settlement, he declared bankruptcy one bleak March morning—the final straw, when he had, as a last resort, turned to the friends who had lived off his largess for so many years . . . and asked for help . . . and discovered that there were none left—*not one.*

Without money for drugs, Charles suffered agonizing withdrawals; his screams could be heard for blocks. The years of dissipation had taken a terrible toll and etched their trail across his face: no one looking at his face would have judged him to be under fifty.

But he still had enough pride left to change his name so as not to further besmirch a name which had never before been dragged in the dust.

Another chicken came home to roost when Charles, a four-pack-a-day chain-smoker, was diagnosed with lung cancer. Thanks to the staff of a London charity hospital, who treated him without remuneration, he pulled through after eighteen months, in the process having lost over fifty pounds.

So he moved into the twilight world of London's down-and-outers, a world of high crime where life is cheap and meals are bought with bodies. A few odd jobs—he had no marketable skills—and begging at Trafalgar Square enabled him to eat once a day. That winter being unusually mild, he slept on the streets and managed to keep going . . . but the following

winter, the worst most people could remember, was another matter entirely. Unable to keep warm, his resistance down, he succumbed to bronchial pneumonia.

One bitterly cold January morning, emaciated, coughing, and wheezing, Charles stood outside Buckingham Palace and thought back to the wedding of Prince Charles and Lady Diana. As a cousin of the prince, he had been a guest of the Windsors during the wedding festivities; ruefully he looked down at his tattered clothes and unkempt beard and wondered what the royal family would think if they could see him now.

In sheer desperation, he turned and began walking out of the city. No one who saw this bony bundle of rags could possibly have recognized here the person the press had labelled "the playboy of the Western world."

Unless he found food and warmth somewhere, he knew that he would be dead in a matter of days.

How far he walked . . . and for how many days and nights . . . he never knew. *All* he knew was that he woke up one morning in a haystack. Neither did he ever know how long he stayed there before the wracking fever chills began to leave him

He had been discovered one bone-chillingly cold morning by an extremely irritable farmer, who permitted him to stay only because of the pleas of his wife . . . on *one* condition: that he would feed and care for the hogs—and that he would have to eat what *they* ate.

In the icy, snowy nightmare weeks and months

that followed, he lived on slop—and an occasional glass of milk or piece of bread surreptitiously slipped to him by the farmer's sympathetic wife.

Then the rains came. He thought they would never stop. Rarely, as he moved through the standing water and muck, was he ever dry. His beard matted, his body filthy and encumbered with lice—he had forgotten when he last had a bath—with only one pair of pants, one shirt, and one pair of shoes (with holes in the soles letting in water and muck with every step)—none of which had been washed or cleaned since the previous fall—the stench was, understandably, awful. But he was beyond caring; he moved and lived in a twilight world of slow motion—he had lost all track of time and reality in this hoggish hell.

Then . . . at long last . . . the rains stopped, and the sun came out—he had almost forgotten what the sun looked like. He walked out to the canal, stripped, bathed, washed his clothes and hung them on a branch to dry. Earlier that day, he had heard the farmer ask his wife what day it was. The answer, April 28, stunned him . . . his fortieth birthday! For the first time in years, he began to think rationally and take stock of who and what he now was. In the clear light of this welcome spring day, he realized that he was an absolute and total failure. Now divested of money, drugs, liquor, tobacco, false friends, and lovers, he confronted his inner self with the demoralizing truth that *no one* cared whether he lived or died.

And he looked ahead and *despaired*. He had no skills; the world had passed him by during the past nineteen years . . . no present and no future—his entire worldly estate was drying on a willow branch! Flesh and blood could stand no more; he broke down and cried like an orphaned child.

When reality intruded upon him in the shape of evening shadows, for the first time in years Charles thought of home. *Home*, which he had traded away for money, mica instead of gold. He thought of Robert. Had he married? Were there any children? . . . And Mother . . . did she care? And Father . . . once the anchor of his world . . .

His thoughts, interspersed with gnawing hunger pangs, now gave him no rest, as memories of his childhood and youth thundered up the coasts of his mind. Belatedly, he now realized that his father had made up for his wife's frequent—and long—absences with a double dose of love and caring. Dad had been, unbeknownst to him, the Gibraltar of his world. Was Father still alive?

Why not go home—if there still was a home—and beg for a job as a servant, chauffeur, butler, groom? *Any* job would be better than this!

Within hours, he had made his adieus and started walking toward London. A few days later, he stowed away on an outbound freighter. When he was discovered, the ship's captain was kinder than he deserved and allowed him to work for his food. Almost a year later, the ship docked in New York City.

During the long months on the high seas, what a thrill it had been to feel his strength flowing back. He had lost all interest in drugs, liquor, tobacco, or one-night relationships. He was going *home* . . . and he refused to face his father until he could again look him in the eye.

He couldn't wait to get out of New York City, for his values had changed. Somewhere on the shoals of the nightmare years, godless materialism had ceased to be his all in all, and he had felt the presence of the God of his childhood: like Francis Thompson's "Hound of Heaven," he had sensed this divine pursuit across the trackless oceans, and now this presence dogged his every step.

Convinced that he needed more time before facing his father, instead of using the $100 parting gift from the thoughtful sea captain for a plane ticket, he decided to walk the several hundred miles home. His months on ship had deepened his childhood romance with the sea; thus it was that his journey south meandered down the coast of New Jersey. Whenever possible, he took off his now almost completely useless shoes and walked down the long beaches, listening with joy to the sounds and smells of God's creation: the raucous calls of the gulls, the crashing of the breakers, the inimitable scents and sounds of the eternal romance of sea and sand.

At Cape May, he spent almost all the money he had left for a ferry ticket across to the Delaware side. Then he continued, but now the sounds and sights of civilization again jarred upon his reveries—before he got to Ocean City, he turned inland. Just after he crossed the wide Choptank River, he happened to look back and saw what looked like a weighted sack being heaved (from the back of a passing pickup) out into the river. On a hunch, Charles ran back to the water's edge, dove in, and caught it before it sank out of sight. When he opened the sack, he discovered one very wet and terrified half-grown kitten. Charles adopted him, and from that time they foraged toward Baltimore together.

Meanwhile, the world had not stood still on the Huntington estate. Mrs. Huntington had been killed by a drunk driver two years earlier. Robert had married into one of Boston's oldest and wealthiest families; he and Elizabeth had two children. Robert, always civic minded, was currently United Way President for the annual fund drive, was East Coast coordinator for the Johns Hopkins Cancer Center fund drives, and was head deacon at Washington's National Cathedral. Robert and his father had lost heavily in silver (with the Hunt brothers) and even more heavily in their petroleum and Southwest real estate ventures; nevertheless, because of astute investments elsewhere, the family's net assets still approached $7 billion. As for the now silver-headed Marshall, he had moved his corporate headquarters to Round Bay a number of years ago. Out of his office window, he could look down the half-mile drive to the gate and the scenic roadway below.

During the almost two decades since the memorable day when Marshall had lost his youngest son, Charles had never been far from his daily thoughts and concerns. During Charles's playboy years, he easily kept track of his son's whereabouts, but when the crash came and gossip and society columnists turned elsewhere, he lost contact. When the news of his son's bankruptcy reached him, he immediately sent one of his top aides to London with an offer of economic assistance; but his son was not to be found. Subsequently, he secured the services of a worldwide detective agency and asked them to find his son, no matter what the cost might be. As the years passed, these detective searches continued, but not a shred of a clue as to his son's existence surfaced; it was as if the earth had swallowed him up. Lately, Robert had become increasingly vocal about the mounting detective tab (over $100 million), but Marshall refused to give up the search.

With Charles gone, with his wife's death, with the death of his only brother, loneliness settled upon Marshall like a pall—why even Genghis had breathed his last, leaving the vast study lonelier than ever.

Several times each hour, the father would find himself looking down the drive to the bay . . . but hour after hour, day after day, week after week, month after month, and year after weary year passed—and still no Charles. Robert often ridiculed Marshall and told him that of *course* Charles was dead—if he had needed money, he most certainly would have been back to mooch on them years ago! But somehow, the father felt that Charles was still alive . . . somewhere . . . and he yearned to see him once more before he died.

Today was one of those absolutely perfect Severn

River June days that bridge the heart-stopping beauty of the dogwood, cherry blossoms, and rainbow-hued azaleas of spring with the shimmering greens, returning gulls, and sultry heat of summer. Marshall had awakened earlier than usual, arose, dressed, and sat down on the east veranda to watch the sunrise. After breakfast he went into the study and tried to work, but his thoughts continually played truant and strayed to the long driveway.

Just before noon he again looked down the road to the water's edge and saw a figure talking to the gatekeeper. The gatekeeper let the figure through.

Slowly the figure inched up the long hill.

Gradually the figure became more distinct. Marshall reached for his binoculars . . . something familiar about that *walk*. Suddenly, he *knew!* He leaped out of his chair, knocked over a priceless Ming vase, and ignoring its shattering, ran for the door—almost tripping over his dumbfounded secretary—dashed down the steps, and sprinted down the hill.

Meanwhile, Charles had begun to slow his steps. What if his father refused to see him? *Why should* he wish to see him? What if his father was dead? . . . Slower yet, his steps. Suddenly, he noticed a far-off figure running towards him. Was he about to be thrown off the premises as a trespasser? . . . He stopped, rooted in fear and despair . . . then he recognized the runner . . . and his heart stood still.

When Charles could at last read his father's face, relief washed over him. By this time, the servants and corporate employees had streamed out of the mansion to see what had caused the boss to run down the road as if his life were at stake. They saw two men—one in tattered clothes—hugging each other . . . and those with binoculars saw the tears.

After the storm of their meeting subsided a little, Charles cleared his throat and started to ask for a job as a servant, a groom, a butler, a chauffeur—but each time he began, his father motioned him with his upraised palm to desist. Up the drive to the study they went, sat by the Tiffany window, and the story—not the wild years, but the way back—was told. While the story was being told, the kitten was carefully studying the elder Huntington's face; satisfied with the appraisal, he leaped onto Marshall's lap, stretched out his tired body, and purred like a Pratt-Whitney engine—thus beginning the reign of Genghis Khan II.

The following day, event followed event in rapid succession. Several servants were heard to remark that Marshall looked and acted ten years younger than he had the day before. His personal tailor arrived to measure Charles and begin the process of outfitting him with a new wardrobe; his hair was styled; he was given thorough physical and dental checkups. As for his bedroom, it had been maintained in day-to-day readiness for almost twenty years. About noon, Charles was summoned to the front portico; there, with a huge ribbon across it, was a silver gray Lamborghini. Climaxing the eventful day was the arrival of Marshall's attorney who, after dinner in the Emerald Room, read out loud to Charles the new will, which made both sons equal

heirs to the family fortune. Charles initially refused, declaring that he was unworthy, that he had already spent his half, that . . . but his father refused to let him go on: "The will has nothing to do with worthiness; I make you an equal heir because I wish it so." At this, Charles broke down.

A week later on Saturday evening, the limos of the nation's wealthy and powerful, one by one, were waved through the gate and they wound up the winding drive to the portico, where doormen opened the car doors and escorted the guests into the glittering grand ballroom—unused, at Marshall's express command for almost twenty years. Next day, newspapers across the nation carried the story on the front page, and it was also covered by ABC, CBS, and NBC evening news. *The Washington Post* article began:

Last evening's homecoming of the long-missing—and feared dead—Charles Huntington was like a royal progress. Marshall Huntington, an international power, must really have cashed in his chips . . . because never in our memory have we seen such a crowd of luminaries together for a nonpolitical event in one place on the East Coast. The Who's Who of the nation were there. But the biggest surprise of the evening was when helicopters landed President and Mrs. Bush and Elizabeth and Philip of England with their entourages.

But the most significant event of the evening, in terms of our story, occurred at the height of all the hubbub, right after the presidential and royal parties had entered the grand ballroom. Robert, who had been rafting down the Colorado, hence inaccessible by phone, had suddenly arrived on the scene—and started one of his own. Upon being informed that the festivities were in honor of his brother's return, he exploded and adamantly refused to even go inside. By this time, because of all the commotion Robert was causing, the evening's master of ceremonies felt obliged to interrupt a conversation with the President and summon Marshall outside.

Upon seeing Robert's almost livid face and his obvious fury, Marshall tried to calm him down before the media would pick up this family dissension—but Robert was in no mood to be calmed down and continued to bellow out his frustration and outrage to all within earshot: "Father, I have slaved for you all these years . . . have never once disobeyed your orders, never once brought on you and the family name a shadow of disgrace—yet you have not so much as given my friends and me a small party. . . . But now . . . this worthless son of yours turns up—as I *knew* the skunk would!—after having blown half of *our* fortune on drugs, liquor, prostitutes, and dissipation of all kinds. . . . After *all* this, he has the *gall* to show up with his hand out. . . . And *you*, Father . . . then throw the party of the century for him!"

Through all this tirade, Marshall remained quiet; he just listened.

Finally, this silence broke through to Robert, and he stammered to a stop, wondering if he had gone too far. Marshall walked over to his son, put his arm on his shoulder, and quietly suggested that they retire to the study. Once inside, Marshall, very softly yet firmly responded: "Robert, you just don't seem to understand. Love isn't conditional. This fortune was here before you were born; thus you have not earned it, anymore than any one of our top corporate executives has earned it; each is paid a lucrative monthly salary, and so are you."

More quietly still, he continued, "Yes, you have stayed with me . . . and I deeply appreciate your steadfast devotion to duty. But I do not like to see what greed has done to you and to your relationship with your brother. . . . I'd like you to do some prayerful thinking about the motives which caused your scene tonight. Robert—getting back to the return of your brother—half of all that I have is still yours. . . . How could we *help* celebrating this happy day? Your brother here was dead and has come back to life, was lost and is found."

BELOVED, neither can salvation be earned; it, too, is a gift, a product of love, the deepest and most all-encompassing love in myriads of universes. It is we elder brothers whose yardsticks are miscalibrated.

There is an old hymn with a timeless and rather radical message. I personally feel that these twenty-four lines by Faber perfectly capsulize the story of the Prodigal Son Christ left with us:

There's a wideness in God's mercy,
Like the wideness of the sea;
There's a kindness in His justice,
Which is more than liberty.

There is welcome for the sinner,
And more graces for the good;
There is mercy with the Saviour;
There is healing in His blood.

There's no place where earthly sorrows
Are more felt than up in heav'n;
There's no place where earthly failings
Have such kindly judgment giv'n.

For the love of God is broader
Than the measure of man's mind;
And the heart of the Eternal
Is most wonderfully kind.

But we make His love too narrow,
By false limits of our own;
And we magnify His strictness
With a zeal He will not own.

If our love were but more simple,
We should take Him at His word;
And our lives would be all sunshine
In the sweetness of our Lord.